CANADIAN BOYS WHO ROCKED THE WORLD

Canadian Boys Who Rocked the World

Tanya Lloyd Kyi

Illustrations by Tom Bagley

Walrus Books, an imprint of Whitecap Books

Edited by Viola Funk
Proofread by Sonnet Force and Ben D'Andrea
Illustrations by Tom Bagley
Cover and interior design by Five Seventeen
Typesetting and additional interior design by
Andrea Schmidt/a-schmidt.com and Michelle Mayne

LIBRARY AND ARCHIVES CANADA CATALOGUING IN PUBLICATION

Kyi, Tanya Lloyd, 1973–
Canadian boys who rocked the world / Tanya Lloyd Kyi ;
illustrations by Tom Bagley.

Includes index.
ISBN-10 1-55285-799-9
ISBN-13 978-1-55285-799-1

1. Teenage boys—Canada—Biography—Juvenile literature.
2. Teenage boys—Canada—Attitudes—Juvenile literature.
3. Men—Canada—Biography—Juvenile literature.
4. Canada—Biography—Juvenile literature.
I. Bagley, Tom II. Title.

FC26.Y6K95 2006 J305.235'1092271 C2006-900696-2

The publisher acknowledges the financial support of the Canada Council for the Arts, the British Columbia Arts Council, and the Government of Canada through the Book Publishing Industry Development Program (BPIDP). Whitecap Books also acknowledges the financial support of the Province of British Columbia through the Book Publishing Tax Credit.

The inside pages of this book are 100% recycled, processed chlorine-free paper with 50% post-consumer content. For more information, visit Markets Initiative's website: www.ancientforestfriendly.com.

PRINTED AND BOUND IN CANADA.

In memory of Christopher Oo

CONTENTS

INTRODUCTION

At three years old, Glenn Gould was reading sheet music. He performed in his first concert when he was 12, gave a public recital at 14, and played on CBC Radio at 17. By the time he was 20, he was composing his own works and performing across Canada.

Listeners were amazed at the clarity he brought to piano compositions—even at top speed, he played every note distinctly. As his fame grew, he toured Europe, performed in the Soviet Union during the Cold War, and appeared on television with the New York Philharmonic Orchestra.

But Glenn was never comfortable in the public eye. He insisted on certain rituals—the same chair for every performance, for example, and time to soak his hands before playing. In 1964, he gave his last public performance. Though he continued to work, creating more than 60 recordings, he avoided public appearances and interviews. Instead, he dedicated himself to composing, recording, and creating.

Glenn died after a massive stroke in October 1982, leaving behind a reputation as one of Canada's most eccentric geniuses.

When we think of people who achieve great things in childhood, we often think first of child prodigies: musicians or mathematicians who, like

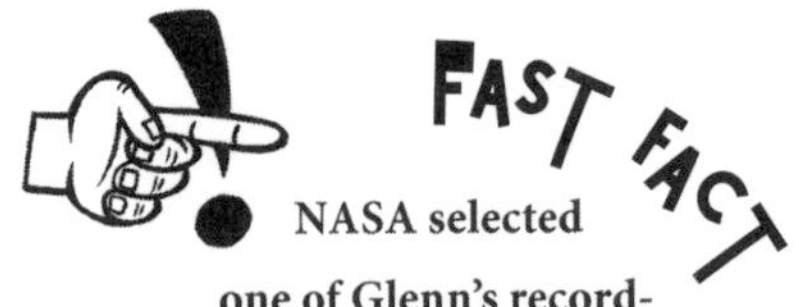

NASA selected one of Glenn's recordings as an example of humankind's greatest achievements on earth. The Prelude and Fugue in C, from Book Two of The Well-Tempered Clavier, was recorded on a gold-plated copper disk and sent into space on the Voyager 1. The vessel is still travelling into space today.

Glenn, are born with phenomenal talent and go on to use their abilities to influence others around the world.

And without a few of these geniuses among us, where would we be? Albert Einstein would never have conceived the Theory of Relativity, Wolfgang Amadeus Mozart would never have composed his masterpieces, and Pablo Picasso would never have begun his Blue Period.

And yet, boys around the world, and throughout Canada, have man-aged to achieve great things without being born geniuses. Some are simply born with strength, determination, and an unstoppable sense of adventure.

In 1784, when he was 14 years old, David Thompson signed on as an apprentice with the Hudson's Bay Company. His father had died before David turned two, and the young boy had spent most of his life in schools for charity cases. The idea of setting off for North America seemed irresistibly exciting, and he couldn't wait to leave London for the New World.

His adventures began almost immediately. After a year at a post on Hudson Bay, David set off on a 240-kilometre (150-mile) trek to York Factory with two native guides. He was 15 years old. In the next five years, he established new fur-trading posts, learned to hunt, studied the Cree language, and researched navigation and astronomy.

By the time he was 20, David was a respected land surveyor in an unmapped country. He became the first white man to travel from the Columbia River's source in the Rocky Mountains to its mouth at the Pacific Ocean. He criss-crossed the prairies, the Rockies, and the Cascades, creating maps so detailed and accurate that they were still used by the Canadian government 100 years later.

Like many of the boys featured in this book, David Thompson went searching for new experiences. He did everything he could to get to some of the world's most isolated and dangerous places, indulging the same sense of adventure that led Sir Edmund Hillary and Tenzing Norgay to the summit of Mount Everest, or Roald Amundsen to the South Pole.

But not all heroes go searching for new opportunities. Sometimes, ordinary people see a need or injustice and feel compelled to act. In the same way that someone might stand up to a bully at school, these people are willing to take charge of a bad situation and fight for change.

In 2004, Free the Children encouraged sponsors to "Adopt a Village" and help provide education, jobs, and health care for families affected by the tsunami in Southeast Asia.

Born in Thornhill, Ontario, in 1982, Craig Kielburger was 12 years old when he happened to see a shocking photo in the newspaper. The image showed a Pakistani child labourer who had been murdered for speaking out about bad working conditions. Horrified to learn that children in other parts of the world could be sold into slavery, Craig gathered his school friends and founded an organization called Free the Children.

Since then, Craig has devoted his time to raising money and awareness. He started by speaking at local schools, and he has now appeared at conferences and protests in more than 40 countries. His organization has grown to include more than a million young people around the world. Together, these members have worked to raise money for over 400 schools and 200,000 health kits. Their clinics and kits have helped about 500,000 people.

Since he founded Free the Children, Craig has written three books about social activism, earned three nominations for the Nobel Peace

Prize, and enrolled in Peace and Conflict Studies at the University of Toronto. In 2006, he won the World Children's Prize, an award known as the "Children's Nobel Prize."

Glenn Gould, David Thompson, and Craig Kielburger lived vastly different lives at different times, but each changed the world in his unique way. Along with the 30 boys featured in the following chapters, they have one thing in common: they didn't wait. Glenn Gould never stopped to say, "I seem to have talent. Maybe when I'm 30 or 40, I'll try playing some Bach." David Thompson never said, "I might explore that river when I get older." And Craig Kielburger never paused to think, "Once I've graduated from university, I should try to help children in need."

Just like everyone else, these boys had studying to do and friends to meet. Yet they managed to pursue their dreams at the same time. And when we look at their amazing accomplishments and read about the achievements of the other boys in this book, we just might find our own inspiration to change the world. After all, what are we waiting for?

BRAWN & BRAINS

ROCKING THE SPORTS WORLD

Louis Cyr

WEIGHTLIFTER

1863-1912

Twelve-year-old Louis Cyr was running through the woods near his hometown of Saint-Cyprien, Quebec, one day, when he came across an injured man. Irénée Gagnon, a land-owner who had been marking his timber for cutting, had twisted his leg.

Irénée ordered the boy to run to the village and bring back help.

Louis shrugged. He could run to the village and back, he said, but it would take several hours. It would be much faster to simply carry the man to safety.

Without listening to Irénée's protests, Louis heaved the man over his shoulders and began walking slowly and carefully to the edge of the trees, where he lowered Irénée onto his wagon.

Astonished by the boy's strength, Irénée arrived at the Cyr family home the following Sunday with a job offer. At 12 years old, Louis left school and embarked on a career of physical labour.

The second of 17 children, Louis was born to a family known for strength. His mother was the largest woman in the neighbourhood, and his grandfather was famous as the most powerful man in the region. Louis adored his grandfather and followed him everywhere, listening to his stories.

"If you are strong, you are everything," the old man said. "If you are not strong, you are nothing."

Louis took his grandfather's words to heart and worked constantly to build his muscles. In the woods, he carried logs by hand for his new landowner boss, sometimes heaving two at a time. At home on the farm, he selected a newborn calf and lifted it every day. As the calf grew, so did Louis's strength. By the time he was 15 years old, he weighed 91 kilograms (200 pounds).

After a few years working in a textile mill and machine shop when his family moved to New England, Louis found himself back in Quebec and newly married. He took a job in a lumber camp, where his strength became legendary. If there was a loaded wagon in his way, Louis would simply brace his feet, lean his shoulder against the back, and move it from the trail.

In 1883, Louis began to travel and perform, astounding audiences throughout Quebec and the Maritimes. He could lift a horse off the ground, balance a platform of 18 men on his back, and push a freight car uphill. Regional strongmen who dared to challenge him were often met with humiliating defeat.

FAST FACT

In one of his demonstrations, Louis lifted a 227-kilogram (500-pound) weight with one finger. The event proved Louis's abilities as a showman more than as a strongman. Today's medical professionals know that people can lift almost the same weight with one finger as they can using their entire hand.

One of these strongmen was David Michaud of Quebec City, a man who hadn't lost a match in 10 years. For his competition with Louis, David chose an event in which each strongman would lift a series of stones, beginning with one that weighed 45 kilograms (100 pounds), and ending with a 226-kilogram (500-pound) boulder. At the end of the line-up was an even larger stone, too heavy for the scales.

The event favoured David; he was used to showcasing such feats of strength. Louis had gained his reputation from more practical demonstrations at the farm or the lumber camp.

BOYS AROUND THE WORLD

Edson Arantes do Nascimento, known to fans as Pelé, was born in Brazil to a family too poor to afford a soccer ball. He and his friends used grapefruits or stuffed socks instead. But by the time he was 15, he was good enough to be offered a place in Brazil's professional soccer league. Two years later, he became the youngest World Cup winner in history. Before he retired in 1977, Pelé had scored over a thousand goals.

Before a cheering crowd, David easily hefted the first stone. Louis did the same, making the lift look a little more difficult than it really was, just for the sake of drama. One by one, the men lifted progressively larger rocks, 91 kilograms (200 pounds), then 136 kilograms (300 pounds), and on until they both successfully heaved a boulder weighing 204 kilograms (450 pounds). Nearing the end of his strength and daunted by Louis's amazing abilities, David decided he would risk everything on one last lift. He skipped the 227-kilogram (500-pound) rock and went straight for the larger, unmarked boulder.

He strained to lift it . . . and failed.

A moment later, Louis heaved the same boulder to shoulder height. His fame as the strongest man in Canada was sealed.

His obvious prowess led to a new job offer in Montreal. Thieves in the city were armed and running rampant. Would Louis join the police force? Louis agreed and was soon making life difficult for the local criminals. So difficult, in fact, that one gang decided to stage an ambush and end Louis's career. They set up a fake fight between two apparently drunken men. When Louis and his partner stepped in to break things up, a dozen thieves emerged from the crowd, wielding knives and axes. Louis's partner called for help before he was fatally wounded. Louis himself took the offensive. Grabbing one of the thieves to use as a human shield, he waded into the mass of bodies, bashing men on either side of him. By the time backup arrived, many of the criminals were already bleeding and were easily taken prisoner.

Louis's career in the police force didn't last long. Soon, he was back on the road, touring Canada, the United States, and Britain. In 1892, a British noble challenged Louis to match the strength of two of his horses. Louis had the harness of a horse tied to each of his arms. He then held the horses at a complete standstill. He was awarded one of the animals as his prize.

Unfortunately, the constant strain of travelling and performing, along with the strongman's legendary appetite, began to damage his heart. By the time Louis was in his late thirties, he was already having circulation problems. He died in Montreal in 1912, at the age of 49. Though the title of "Strongest Man in the World" has since been passed to others, some of Louis's feats have never been equalled.

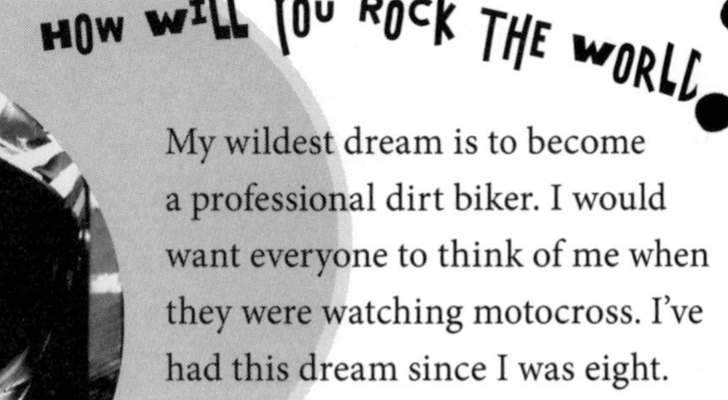

HOW WILL YOU ROCK THE WORLD?

My wildest dream is to become a professional dirt biker. I would want everyone to think of me when they were watching motocross. I've had this dream since I was eight.

— *Gus, age 12*

Elvis Stojko

Skater

1972–

In 1991, Olympia Halle in Munich, Germany, was transformed into a world of ice. Fans crowded around the sideboards and peered down from the top bleachers as the world's most famous skaters competed in the World Figure Skating Championships.

One of the competitors who took to the ice was almost unknown outside of Canada. It was Elvis Stojko, an 18-year-old from Richmond Hill, Ontario. Two years before, he had placed second in the Canadian championships, and he'd also skated in the 1990 world championships. His style, a combination of athletic jumps, dazzling speed, and quick footwork, was less traditionally "artistic" than that of most skaters, and not all judges appreciated it. He wasn't considered a serious medal contender.

Then Elvis did something that made the sports commentators gasp, the fans rise to their feet, and the judges check their spectacles. He performed the first quadruple-double jump combination in competition, rotating four times in the air, then leaping again for two more rotations—and landing in the history books.

"This just goes to show that if you really want it bad enough, you can pull it together," Elvis told reporters.

*

Named after singer Elvis Presley, Elvis grew up loving sports and speed. He started skating when he was four and won his first trophy at age six. In later years, Elvis also practised martial arts and slaked his thirst for adventure with dirt biking, snowmobiling, and jet skiing.

But other sports always had to squeeze between skating practices. Spending early mornings, afternoons, and even late evenings on the ice, Elvis worked to perfect his technique, practising each jump and each footwork combination until he could perform them with absolute confidence.

That kind of focus brought Elvis much success in competition. He won the Canadian championships in 1994, 1996, 1997, 1998, 1999, 2000, and 2002. In between awing hometown crowds, he won gold at the World Figure Skating Championships in 1994, 1995, and 1997, when he performed history's first quadruple-triple jump combination. At the Olympic Games in 1994 and 1998, he earned silver medals.

Since 1994, Elvis has served as a Kids Ambassador for Ronald McDonald Children's Charities, spending time with sick or disabled kids.

At the 1998 Winter Olympics in Nagano, Japan, Elvis impressed fans all over the world, not only with his abilities but with his perseverance. Competing against Russian skater Ilya Kulik—who skated almost perfectly—Elvis managed short and long programs that were technically strong but lacked his usual flamboyant style. Fans found out why when he doubled over in pain after the long program. All week, he'd been hiding a serious groin injury and battling the flu, without strong painkillers because of the anti-drug rules at the Olympics. But Elvis hadn't let either problem keep him from a chance to vie for a prize. Too sore to skate to the podium to receive his silver medal, he walked across the ice in his running shoes.

BOYS AROUND THE WORLD

Russian dancer Mikhail Baryshnikov began studying ballet at the age of nine. Seeing the young man's talent, a professional company hired him at 18, and he began travelling the world as the principal male dancer after only three years. Mikhail later applied for political asylum in the United States, where he danced with the nation's top companies and appeared in several films and television productions.

Fans also loved Elvis because of his dedication to fun. He surprised crowds at the 1994 Canadian championships with a performance set to an Elvis Presley medley, and later skated in an Elvis Presley tribute in Memphis, Tennessee. Martial arts hero Bruce Lee inspired another of the skater's programs.

Elvis found new opportunities to hone both his skills and his fun-loving spirit when he turned to professional skating in 2002. He continues to appear in live performances and television specials around the world.

HOW WILL YOU ROCK THE WORLD?

When I grow up,
I want to drive a
Zamboni and make
the ice really slippery
so that people can
skate really fast!

— Brandon, age 5

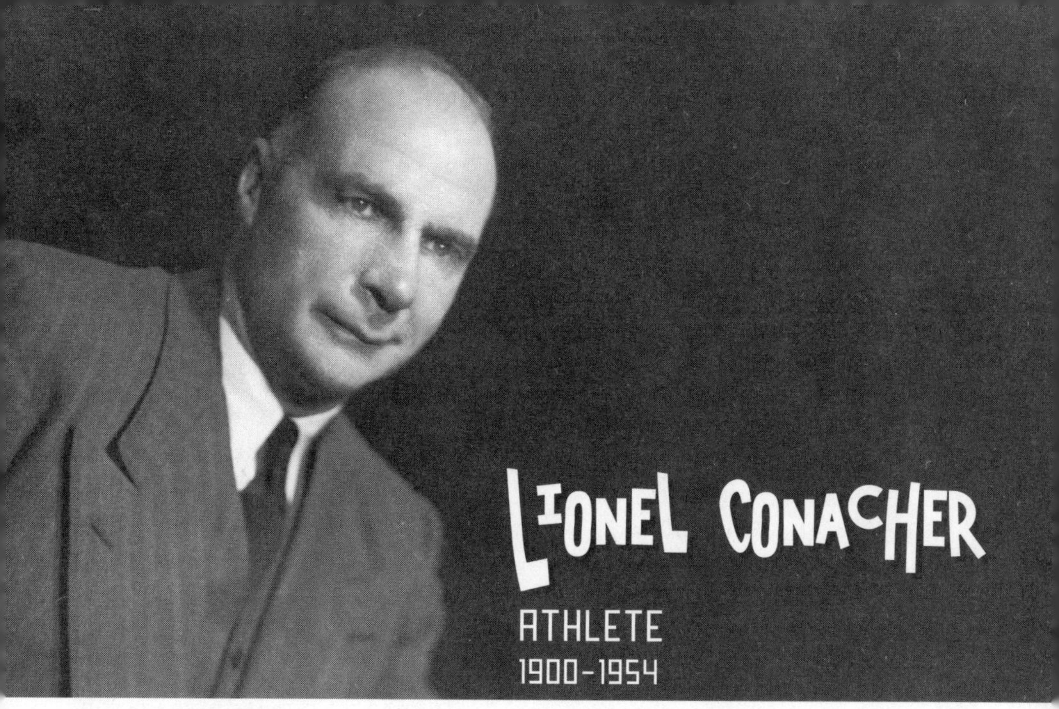

LIONEL CONACHER

ATHLETE

1900–1954

It was the ninth inning and the Toronto Hillcrests baseball team were losing by one run. With the bases loaded, slugger Lionel Conacher stepped to the plate. A pitch, the sharp sound of a hit, and Lionel was off and running, rounding first base and sprinting to second. One, then two Hillcrest players screamed across home plate. Victory!

The crowd went wild, but Lionel barely heard the applause. He was tearing off his Hillcrests jersey and racing toward a waiting taxi. Across town, his lacrosse team was losing 2 to 1. Lionel steamed onto the field and scored two goals—his second game-winning achievement of the afternoon.

Ever since childhood, Lionel had been amazing his friends, coaches, and fans with his athletic abilities. The oldest in a family of 10 children, the boy found his days busy with school and his job loading and delivering sod. But he squeezed in sports wherever he could, whether football on the nearby school fields or road hockey outside his front door. In the winter, he and his brothers would come home from the rink and eat dinner without removing their skates, so they could rush back to the rink as soon as they were finished.

Watching his parents work endless hours to meet the needs of their growing family, Lionel promised himself that he would find a way to escape poverty. As a young teen, the best way he could imagine was to excel at every sport he tried. He played rugby, baseball, and football with neighbourhood teams, and took up boxing and wrestling at the local gym.

A combination of natural talent and determination brought him success. When he was 16, he won the Ontario wrestling championship for his weight class. Three years later, he led two hockey teams to national championships and his football team to the provincial championship. And at 21, he won the light heavyweight boxing championship of Canada.

Lionel's little brother Charlie was a star player for the Toronto Maple Leafs. When they met on the ice, the two brothers would pretend to be bitter rivals, to make the games more exciting for the fans. But sometimes, while they pushed and punched each other, they would actually be chatting about the latest family news.

Football was always Lionel's favourite. In 1921, he joined the Toronto Argonauts, scoring 23 of the team's 27 points in his first game. His technique of plowing straight through the opposing players rather than dancing around them led to his "Big Train" nickname. He quickly became a crowd favourite. And later that year, before a crowd of 10,000 cheering fans, he led the Argonauts to a 23–0 Grey Cup victory.

His dreams of becoming a famous athlete were coming true. And although he wasn't a salaried player, his increasing fame brought money-making opportunities. Businesses would pay him to make an appearance and greet their customers. Lionel and his brother even set up their own laundry business to cash in on his growing reputation.

Lionel was frequently invited to play for professional hockey or baseball teams, but in the 1920s, rules about amateur and professional sports were firm. If he turned professional in one sport, he would no longer be allowed to play as an amateur in any sport. Joining an NHL team, for example, would prevent him from playing on his old football or baseball teams. His refusal to "go pro" led some people to suspect that he was secretly taking money for his sports, but several investigations found him completely innocent.

Finally, in 1923, a sports recruiter found the perfect combination to tempt Lionel. He offered him a place on an amateur hockey team in Pittsburgh (where his fame would draw more fans to the arena), plus a job as an insurance salesman, plus a place at a local preparatory school where he could study for university and play on the football team.

Just before he left for the United States, Lionel eloped with a 17-year-old swimmer named Dorothy Kennedy. Then he turned his attention back to sports and quickly became as successful in Pittsburgh as he had been in Toronto. He was the star player on his school football team and the captain of the Pittsburgh Yellow Jackets hockey team.

But with a young wife and a new family to support, Lionel finally began to think about turning professional. After all, he was 25 years old; his career as an athlete wouldn't last forever. In 1925, he gave up amateur football and became a member of the Pittsburgh Pirates, a National Hockey League team, and the Toronto Maple Leafs baseball team.

Unfortunately, Lionel's greatest rival proved to be alcohol. By the end of the 1920s, his drinking was damaging his performance and making his family life difficult. Determined not to end his career, Lionel stopped drinking altogether and moved back to Toronto to be close to his extended family. Despite constant cravings for alcohol—he would watch endless movies, smoke his pipe, and play marathon rounds of golf to distract himself—he was soon back to being the leading scorer on his hockey team.

In 1932, Lionel went back to the wrestling ring, winning all 26 of his matches that year. To a continent blasted by an economic depression, Lionel was a bright light. He offered constant fun and excitement, and he helped remind people that it was possible to start poor and become wildly successful. Often, there were standing ovations after his wrestling matches.

Boys Around the World

Muhammad Ali won his first professional fight in 1960 when he was 18 years old. In the next three years, the American heavyweight boxer won all 19 of his matches, 15 of them by knockout. *Sports Illustrated* **named him the "Sportsman of the Century" in 1999.**

Throughout the 1930s, Lionel moved from accomplishment to accomplishment, even winning the Stanley Cup in 1934. But a life of sports had taken its toll. Over the years, he'd suffered eight broken noses, numerous broken bones, two knee operations, and a total of 650 stitches. In 1937, it was time to retire.

Lionel later became a Member of Parliament and a successful businessman. He died of a heart attack at age 54, while playing in an exhibition baseball game. To many of his long-time fans, it seemed fitting that Lionel died while doing what he loved best.

How Will You Rock the World?

I can rock the world by becoming a hockey player. Then I will donate $6 million to the poor and help save the trees.

— Adam, age 7

RICK HANSEN

WHEELCHAIR ATHLETE

1957–

Rick Hansen was fishing by himself at a secluded creek near Abbotsford, BC, when he slid down a bank and into the water. His wheelchair landed on top of him.

After scrambling to the shore and grabbing the wheelchair before it could sink, he found himself at the base of a high bank of slimy mud. There was no one around to help, so he set out to climb it, clutching at roots and grabbing bunches of grass until he collapsed at the top.

He was soaking wet, covered in slime, and exhausted, but not quite ready to head home. He wanted to prove to himself that he could achieve things on his own, and to Rick that meant not giving up when the day became difficult. Wheeling himself to a more stable position along the creek, he grabbed his rod again and cast for a few more fish.

The same courage and perseverance that drove him to keep fishing that afternoon would one day keep him wheeling his way around the world on the Man In Motion World Tour.

When they were 15 years old, Rick and a friend hitched a ride in the bed of a pickup truck on their way home from a fishing trip in northern BC. The driver lost control and skidded off the road, throwing the boys from

BOYS AROUND THE WORLD

When Rick Hansen set off around the world in 1985, he was inspired by another Canadian hero, Terry Fox. After being diagnosed with cancer at 19, Terry underwent several years of treatment, including the amputation of a leg. In 1980, he dipped his artificial leg in the waters off Newfoundland and began an epic cross-country run. After 143 days, the return of his cancer forced him to abandon the run near Thunder Bay, Ontario. Today, millions of people participate in an annual Terry Fox Run, the world's largest one-day cancer fundraiser.

the truck. Although his friend was relatively unscathed, Rick landed on a toolbox below a mountain of debris. When he regained consciousness, Rick couldn't move his legs. He would soon discover that he had injured his spinal cord.

After an operation to fuse some of the bones of his spine together, Rick spent two months in the orthopedic ward of a Vancouver area hospital. He then moved to a rehabilitation centre for three more months of strength work and physiotherapy.

One day, determined to learn as much as possible about his condition, Rick snuck into the nursing station. When he pulled his file from the cabinet, he read "acute paralysis." His back had been broken in not one, but two places, and there was no hope that he'd walk again. A wheelchair would be his primary mode of transportation.

Rick dedicated himself to becoming as quick and stable as possible in his wheelchair and to practising standing with the use of leg braces and crutches. He honed his skills constantly, even clambering up and down the stairs after all the therapists had gone home. When he returned to his family's home in Williams Lake, BC, he continued to push himself to improve. Soon, he was wheelchair dancing at school functions, coaching volleyball, and playing sports.

At 18, he played table tennis in the 1975 Canadian Wheelchair Games in Montreal. The trip gave him the opportunity to see the range of sports played by people with disabilities. By the time he was 19, Rick was enrolled in the University of British Columbia on his way to a degree in physical education. He was playing wheelchair basketball (and introducing Terry Fox to the sport), as well as coaching. His volleyball team won the Canadian Wheelchair Games that year, and his basketball team placed fifth at the World Games.

But Rick was about to find his niche—in the track and field stadium. He was soon immersed in training, even helping to design his own racing wheelchair, and his efforts led to a third place finish in the Vancouver Marathon. Then, at the 1980 world championship wheelchair marathon, he shocked himself and the rest of the world by crossing the finish line 14 minutes ahead of the other competitors.

Inspired by his marathon successes and by his friend Terry Fox, Rick began to develop a wild idea. What if he wheeled his way around the world to raise awareness and money for spinal cord research? When he began planning the tour, Rick had no idea how much energy—and how much of his life—it would eventually eat up. But in 1985, he and his team gathered with crowds of supporters in a Vancouver mall, before setting off toward the United States border on the first part of his journey.

Rick's journey around the world took two years, two months, and two days. He received more than 200,000 letters of support along the way.

After one year, he'd had 63 flat tires, worn out 47 pairs of gloves, and used 100 rolls of athletic tape. He'd pushed his wheels about 7,180,800 times, and one of his chairs had disintegrated under the strain. By the end of two years, Rick had wheeled for more than 40,000 kilometres (25,000 miles), through 34 countries, and raised over $26 million.

When he returned home, Rick created the Man In Motion Foundation to continue raising funds and awareness. The millions of dollars collected since the tour help improve the day-to-day lives of people with spinal cord injuries and related disabilities.

Rick now lives in Richmond, BC, with his wife and three daughters.

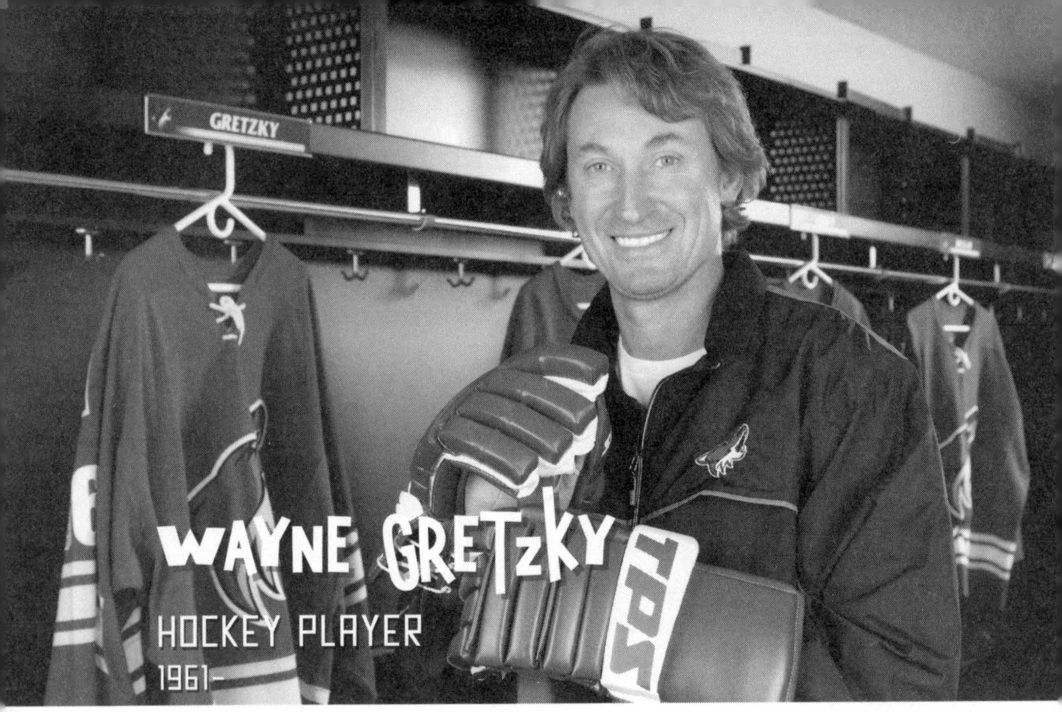

WAYNE GRETZKY

HOCKEY PLAYER

1961–

Six-year-old Wayne Gretzky climbed into his dad's car after the year-end hockey league banquet, and promptly burst into tears. When his dad asked him what the matter was, Wayne stammered, "Everyone won a trophy but me."

His dad wasn't fazed. "Wayne, keep practising and one day you're gonna have so many trophies, we're not gonna have room for them all."

Wayne's dad was right. He knew his son well, and he knew how dedicated Wayne was to the sport. In fact, Wayne played so often at the nearby outdoor rink that his dad eventually flooded the family's backyard, set up floodlights, and invited the local kids over to play. As long as the cold weather lasted—and in Brantford, Ontario, it lasted quite a while—Wayne would skate for an hour each morning, then rush home after school to skate until bedtime, taking the shortest dinner break possible.

He was so addicted to hockey that when he was six years old, he and his dad convinced the local children's team (usually restricted to 10-year-olds) to let him audition. In his first year, Wayne struggled to keep up with the larger boys. But when he was seven, he scored 27 goals. A year later, his total was 104, then 196 the next year. When he was 10 years old and

BOYS AROUND THE WORLD

Russian hockey player Vladislav Aleksandrovich Tretiak started playing goal in exchange for a popular hockey jersey—no one else on the team wanted the position. He was named to the Soviet Ice Hockey League's All-Star team when he was 19. A year later, he helped his team win a gold medal at the 1972 Winter Olympics. He earned two more Olympic golds and 10 world championships before hanging up his skates in 1984. More recently, he served as the goal-tender coach for the Chicago Blackhawks.

barely taller than the net, he scored 378 goals in 69 games, outscoring every other player in the league by more than 200 goals.

Suddenly, Wayne was famous. He was interviewed by a national magazine and appeared on a 30-minute television show. People even began asking for his autograph. When he was 14, Wayne was invited to play for a junior hockey team in Toronto. It meant leaving home, living with someone else's family, and playing with men much older than him, but he leapt at the chance.

In 1977, the World Junior Hockey Championships were held in Montreal and Wayne was there, the youngest player on the ice. In six games, he managed eight goals and nine assists, raising the eyebrows of hockey scouts from across the continent. Soon, he'd signed a four-year contract with the World Hockey Association's Indianapolis Racers for almost a million dollars. Only a few months later, he was traded to the Edmonton Oilers.

FAST FACT

Along the way to hockey stardom, Wayne married an actress named Janet Jones and had five children.

Wayne was hailed as one of history's most talented players, but he was also one of hockey's hardest workers. Even during the busiest times of the season, he practised constantly, always looking for new ways to improve his game.

On January 26, 1979, Wayne's 18th birthday, the owner of the Oilers had a giant cake shaped like a 99—Wayne's jersey number—pushed to centre ice. Amid cheers and fanfare, Wayne signed a contract for $3 million over 10 years. He went on to lead the league in scoring and win the Rookie of the Year trophy.

That was only the beginning of Wayne's award-winning career. Soon, he would prove his father right and earn more trophies than would fit in the family living room. During the 1981–82 season, he broke Maurice Richard's record of 50 goals in 50 games by scoring 50 goals in 39 games. By the end of the year, he'd totalled an amazing 92 goals and 120 assists in 80 games.

Wayne played with the Oilers for nine years before he was traded to the Los Angeles Kings. After short stints with the St. Louis Blues and the New York Rangers, he finally stepped off the NHL ice in 1999, leaving a string of records behind him. He had won nine most valuable player awards, set 15 playoff records, and won four Stanley Cups. For being the most gentlemanly player on the ice, he was awarded five Lady Byng Memorial trophies. He was also known for being a team player with an incredible sense of where his teammates were on the ice. Along with his scoring records, he broke the record for most assists: 163 in a season.

When six-year-old Wayne started playing on a league team, his jersey was so big that it would catch on his stick. His dad tucked the right side of the jersey into his pants, and Wayne wore it that way for the rest of his career.

When he retired from the ice, Wayne embarked on a career in hockey management, acting as the executive director for the Canadian men's Olympic hockey team and as managing partner of the Phoenix Coyotes. He was inducted into the Hockey Hall of Fame on November 22, 1999.

WICKED WARRIORS

ROCKING THE WARTIME WORLD

Alan Arnett McLeod

Air Force Pilot

1899–1918

High above the ground and well inside enemy airspace, Alan Arnett McLeod arced his bomber in a tight circle, giving his flying partner Arthur Hammond a clear shot at the German plane chasing them. Arthur let loose three sharp bursts of gunfire. The German plane flipped. Then it was spinning. Within an instant, it had smashed into the ground far below. Alan shouted in triumph. It was the thick of the action in World War I, he was 18 years old, and he was doing something he'd dreamed about for the last four years. He was flying a fighter plane. And he was very very good at it.

Just then, his bomber burst through cloud cover into the open sky above. Immediately, eight German triplanes dove toward him, already firing. Dipping and diving, slowing, then speeding up, Alan used every maneuver he knew to dodge the enemy bullets and give Arthur a chance to aim the gun. Soon, bullets ripped one of the triplanes almost in half, and it burst into flames.

But Alan couldn't out-fly seven planes forever. An enemy dove underneath him, peppering his bomber with bullets. Both Alan and Arthur were hit, the gas tank burst into flames, and the floor in the front of their plane dropped away. Amazingly, Alan managed to hurl himself onto the wing of the aircraft, reaching back inside the cockpit to steer with one arm. Meanwhile, Arthur kept a tight grip on the gun, shooting down a second German plane. Then he, too, jumped out onto the wing just as the bomber smashed into a shell hole on the ground.

Since he was a child, Alan had dreamed of serving in the military. When he was 14, he convinced recruiters to let him join two weeks of military training at Fort Sewell. The rest of the soldiers were at least 18 years old.

The Victoria Cross is the most prestigious award given for bravery in the British Commonwealth. Only 94 Canadians have ever received one.

When World War I began, Alan couldn't wait to get on the battlefield. He tried to enlist when he was 15, then again when he was 17. Both times he was sent home, too young. But on his 18th birthday, Alan said goodbye to his high school class in Stonewall, Manitoba, and left for training in Toronto. Six weeks later, he was in a plane for the first time. Less than two weeks after that, he was flying by himself. And within two months, he was a qualified fighter pilot.

Alan quickly made a name for himself in the skies over Europe, gunning down an observation balloon, taking out German gun posts, and snapping aerial photographs of the enemy lines. When he was paired with Arthur, an observer and gunner who had already won a Military Cross for bravery, the team became one of the most dangerous forces in the sky.

After their battle with the German planes, Alan and Arthur found themselves sprawled on the ground, miraculously alive. Arthur had taken six bullets, and lay unable to move. Alan had also been shot—five times. And when he listened to the surrounding machine-gun fire, he understood that they had crashed in the most dangerous place possible. They were right between the front lines of a battle, with guns firing from both directions.

Boys Around the World

Alexander the Great was in charge of the armies of Macedonia when he was only 16. By the time he died in Babylon in 323 BC, he had squashed a revolt in Greece, conquered Persia, and invaded India. He remains one of history's most successful military leaders.

The plane's gas tank was still burning. Worried that the ammunition on board would soon explode, Alan crawled over to Arthur and began to heave his partner toward the British lines. Again they were injured, this time by a bomb exploding nearby. Still, Alan continued crawling. After what must have seemed like hours, the men drew close enough to the British trenches for soldiers to rush out and haul them to safety. Near to death himself, Alan had nonetheless managed to save his partner's life.

Alan was awarded the Victoria Cross for his bravery and loyalty. After several months recovering in a London hospital, he was invited to Buckingham Palace to receive his award.

He returned home to Stonewall, Manitoba, in September 1918. Tragically, his body was still weak from his wounds, and he couldn't battle the influenza epidemic raging through Canada at the time. He died in a Winnipeg hospital on November 6.

TECUMSEH

NATIVE CHIEF
1768–1813

Leading 200 American soldiers, Major Thomas Van Horne rode toward Brownstown near the Detroit River, eager to join the battles of the War of 1812. The men marched confidently toward the creek at the northern edge of town. They were about to be greeted as heroes, arriving with mail, supplies, and reinforcements.

But Tecumseh, a Shawnee warrior and chief, had other plans. He had only a quarter of the men that Van Horne had, but he had scouted the area well. Quickly, he dispersed his warriors around the creek. Some he hid in the cornfield to the right. Others he sent into the nearby woods. A few he placed in the thick brush by the creek's edge.

Van Horne's men marched closer. Closer.

Suddenly, with a piercing yell, Tecumseh signalled the attack. His men began to fire from all sides. They aimed first for the horses; the animals collapsed, squealing, under their riders.

Again Tecumseh yelled, and his warriors answered with a deafening mix of voices and gunfire from all sides of the American troops. The Americans had no idea how many men were attacking, or from where they were firing. Within minutes, Van Horne's soldiers were on the run, scattering in all directions.

At the end of the ambush, Tecumseh had lost one man. Two more were wounded. But he had killed 20 Americans, wounded a dozen more, and captured the mail. The American lines of communication were once again in jeopardy, and Tecumseh had led yet another successful raid for the British.

Tecumseh was born in a Shawnee village along the Scioto River, in what is now Ohio. As a child, when he should have been creating mischief in the village or learning the basics of hunting, Tecumseh's life was enveloped by war. A tidal wave of settlers from the American colonies was pushing further and further into traditional native lands. By the time he was 14, Tecumseh had seen his people's villages burned by American troops. He had seen native warriors killed by Americans, and American soldiers tortured and scalped by natives. He had seen the body of his father carried back to the village after a brave but unsuccessful attack against American troops.

It's no wonder that the young Tecumseh dedicated himself to becoming a warrior. Already a little taller than average and strikingly handsome, Tecumseh grew lean and strong. He spent his days hunting, proving his bravery, and practising every known form of warfare. At the age of 18, he was riding into gunfire.

His first battle was heartbreaking. In October 1786, American forces pushed across the Ohio River into Shawnee territory, killing the few men who were not away hunting, and capturing women and children. One of the prisoners was an old man named Moluntha, a chief who had cautioned the young warriors of his tribe against violence and battle. Moluntha offered no resistance and was trying to negotiate with the soldiers, but one colonel was convinced that the old man had been involved in an earlier ambush. The colonel grabbed an axe and killed and scalped the chief. To the native tribes of the area, it was a stark sign—making peace with the Americans wouldn't work.

Tecumseh is believed to have chased after the retreating Americans with members of his family, but the natives were hopelessly outnumbered. They could do little but harass and skirmish the troops as the

Americans laid waste to six more villages, taking prisoners as they went. Tecumseh saw women and children marched out of his lands as prisoners, and there was nothing he could do.

Determined to stop the Americans from claiming even more land, Tecumseh joined his people in raids against the new settlers. Waiting in ambush along the banks of the major rivers, they preyed on the flat-bottomed boats that carried immigrants and their supplies. With fierce yells, they would leap from the bushes, overtake the flimsy vessels, kill or capture the passengers, and claim the supplies as their own.

On one raid, Tecumseh saw an American pulled from the river and tortured, burned alive by the native warriors. He didn't interfere—after all, he wasn't the oldest or the most experienced of the group—but he spoke with his people afterwards. Soon, they agreed that no future prisoners would be tortured. And women and children would be left alive.

Tecumseh's ability to persuade his fellow warriors was a sign of his growing leadership abilities. As he became a young man, he earned respect for his planning and intelligence as well as his bravery. He was also unusually generous. While other warriors kept their loot for themselves and their families, Tecumseh distributed his among his people. By 1795, the people had chosen Tecumseh as a chief.

His success didn't mean that Tecumseh lived a more peaceful life. Together with his brother, a popular spiritual leader known as the Prophet, Tecumseh dreamed of uniting all native peoples from Canada to Mexico. To many, it seemed like a ridiculously ambitious idea. Different native nations lived in distant parts of the vast continent and spoke different languages. How could they be united?

Tecumseh believed that native people had to stop selling and trading their traditional lands to the Americans and the British. He knew that free access to the land for hunting and fishing was necessary for the survival of his culture, and he was convinced that the land was the common property of all native people. One band or tribe should not be able to sell or trade land to the British or the Americans

BOYS AROUND THE WORLD

As a Russian high school student in the 1950s, Vladimir Bukovsky started an underground newspaper mocking the government. He was arrested and banned from school, but he managed to forge his way into an alternate school and, eventually, the University of Moscow. As he continued to protest the government, he was arrested, beaten, and imprisoned in a psychiatric hospital. Forced to leave Russia, he spent the rest of his life campaigning against the use of psychological torture.

without the approval of all the other native people.

But while Tecumseh was travelling in the south, building support for his vision of a native union, American troops attacked the village that he and his brother had established. By the time Tecumseh received the news, the settlement had been destroyed and Tecumseh's dream of a continental native union began to crumble.

Sometimes, it must have seemed to Tecumseh that his older brother was right in 1779, when he had written him a letter about war with white settlers:

> *When an Indian is killed, it is a great loss which leaves a gap in our people and a sorrow in our heart; when a white is killed, three or four others step up to take his place and there is no end to it. The white man seeks to conquer nature, to bend it to his will and to use it wastefully until it is all gone and then he simply moves on, leaving the waste behind him and looking for new places to take. The whole white race is a monster who is always hungry and what he eats is land.*

Despite the destruction of his village, Tecumseh refused to despair. He began to see the British as the only hope of preserving some of his people's traditional lands and culture. If the hunting grounds of the south couldn't be saved, maybe he could help preserve those of the north, in what was then Upper Canada. He moved north and gathered his warriors around him.

As the Americans marched on Upper Canada in 1814, hoping to gain more land for the young United States, Tecumseh used his followers to harass and ambush the American troops until the leader of the American forces became convinced that thousands of native warriors must be fighting against him, converging from all sides.

In reality, Tecumseh's forces were few, and constantly outnumbered. They were experts at sneak attacks, but in all-out battle, the Americans had the advantage.

In 1813, in a battle to protect what would later become part of Ontario, Tecumseh was charging forward, yelling to inspire his men, when an American soldier raised his musket. He fired at close range. And Tecumseh fell. The famous leader died in battle, just as he had once promised to do.

With the continued help of native fighters, the British eventually managed to push the Americans back in the War of 1812. And while Tecumseh's dream of a united native presence in North America was never realized, his reputation for bravery and great leadership has lasted for centuries. Americans consider him one of history's greatest native leaders, and Canadians consider him a hero who helped to save the country.

No one knows who killed Tecumseh, although an American soldier-turned-politician later claimed credit for his death. The location of his grave is also a mystery. Some historians say that Canadian troops took the body back to Sandwich, Ontario, with them. Others say the body was secretly buried by Tecumseh's followers, and the gravesite never revealed.

THOMAS RICKETTS

SOLDIER
1901–1967

Tommy Ricketts staggered through the mud of World War I with the rest of his troopmates. Many of the men looked exhausted, tired from the seemingly endless march through the swampy fields of Belgium, and stunned from the noise of the constant gunfire.

Suddenly, the gunfire was closer. Too close. Soldiers on both sides were already falling as Tommy and the others dove for the ground. A heavily armed German troop had materialized in the field in front of them. There was nothing to do but fire back, again and again, and try to keep the enemy soldiers from creeping nearer.

As more men fell, Tommy's commander decided they couldn't simply out-shoot the Germans. If they had any chance, they would have to take the offensive. He asked for a volunteer to accompany him with a machine gun as he tried to creep to the side of the German troop and capture a gun battery there.

Tommy immediately volunteered. Firing constantly, he and his commander began to sprint across the battle lines, running, then diving for cover, then running again. Shells hit the ground around his feet, but Tommy ignored them.

Then, with the length of three football fields between themselves and the gun battery, Tommy and his commander ran out of ammunition.

FAST FACT

Tommy's Victoria Cross was donated to the Canadian War Museum by his widow and is now on display in Ottawa.

The Germans noticed the pause in the rain of bullets, and they began to move closer.

Without stopping to think, Tommy began dashing back toward the nearest friendly soldiers. Again, bullets and shells exploded into the earth around him. He zigzagged his way through, grabbed an armful of ammunition, and repeated his sprint back to his commander. Once the machine gun was reloaded, Tommy paused to take careful aim at each one of the advancing gun teams, forcing them into retreat. The first German gun battery was won.

Eventually, the enemy troop took cover among the buildings of a local farm, and Tommy's platoon was able to advance without anyone else being wounded. They captured five field guns and four machine guns. They also managed to capture eight of the retreating German soldiers.

Tommy might have grown up to be a fisher like his dad if World War I hadn't drawn him away from his home in Middle Arm, Newfoundland. But at 15, he was eager to find adventure. He travelled to St. John's and enlisted with the Royal Newfoundland Regiment.

BOYS AROUND THE WORLD

Forced to quit school to support his family, American Eddie Rickenbacker found work in a machine shop, where he discovered a love of auto racing. He was soon competing on international tracks. But when the United States entered World War I in 1917, he signed up for flight school and became the country's "Ace of Aces," shooting down 26 enemy planes. He flew again in World War II and survived 24 days stranded without food when his plane crashed in the Pacific.

Three months after Tommy's heroic bullet-dodging run in Belgium, Britain's King George V personally awarded him with the Victoria Cross, introducing him as the youngest medal-winner in the army. He was only 17.

After the war, he returned home, studied pharmacy, and opened his own business in St. John's, Newfoundland. He died in 1967. A plaque on the wall of the building where his pharmacy once stood commemorates his achievements in the war.

HOW WILL YOU ROCK THE WORLD?

To rock the world, I would be the first Canadian to be president of the United States.

I have dual citizenship, so I could do it. This would give me the power to change the world.

— Ben, age 12

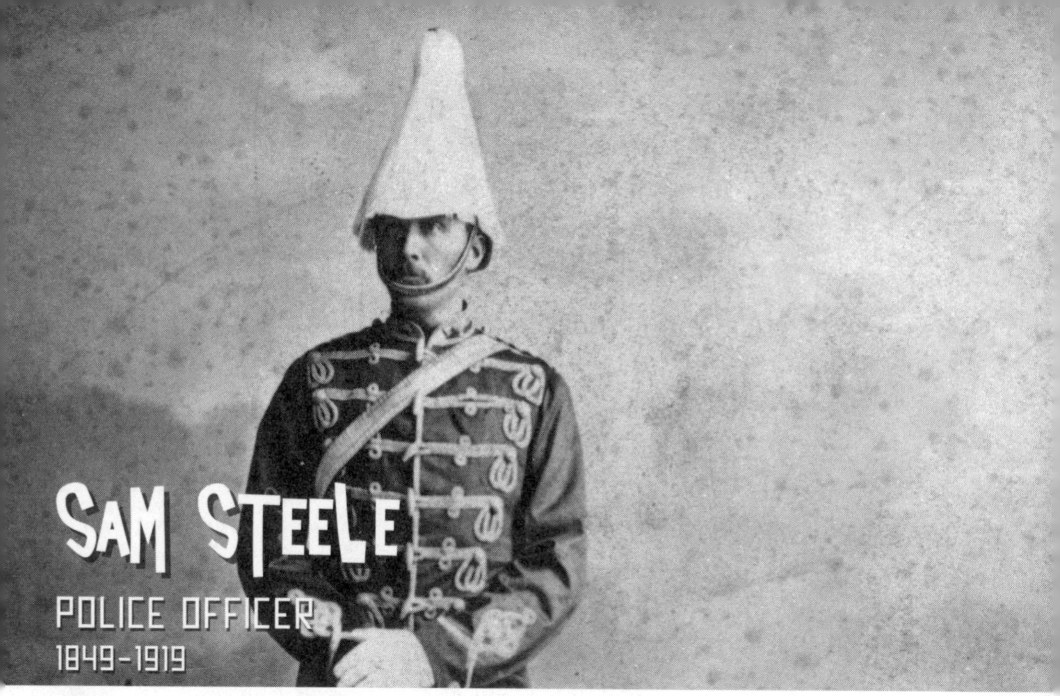

Sam Steele

Police Officer

1849–1919

Sam Steele sank thankfully into his blankets. For weeks, he and some of the first recruits of Canada's new North West Mounted Police force had been marching west through mud and freezing rain. They were finally approaching Fort Edmonton.

Suddenly, a cry rang through the camp. One of the horses was in trouble! Grabbing a rope, Sam raced to the site of the panic. A pack horse had broken through the ice along the banks of Rat Creek. Throwing one end of the rope to his men, Sam slung the other end around the hindquarters of the horse. But just as he was about to give the order to pull, more of the ice broke off. In an instant, several of the men were under the ice, thrashing along with the horse.

Fortunately, none of the young police officers let go of the rope. With heave after heave, Sam and the men on shore pulled them hand-over-hand to safety. Then they pulled in the horse.

Sam's men went to bed, exhausted. They awoke in the morning to find that their leader had never slept. He had spent the rest of the night cutting poles to create a bridge over the creek, eager to have his troops make their way on the last leg of their journey.

The son of a military man, Sam grew up with a keen sense of adventure. At 14, he convinced militia recruiters in Orillia, Ontario, that he was two years older. Soon, he was taking officer training in Toronto. He took a few years off during peacetime, then, at 19, joined the militia to fight the Métis rebellion led by Louis Riel. And when Canada established its own army, taking over from the British soldiers who had served in the past, Sam was the 23rd person to enlist.

Despite his love of the army, Sam still felt an urge to go places army life wouldn't take him. So when Canada established the North West Mounted Police force in 1873, Sam signed up—a decision that would fill the rest of his life with adventure, challenge, and danger. His goal: establish order in western Canada.

The land Sam patrolled would one day become Saskatchewan, Alberta, and British Columbia, but at the time, it was the Wild West. Ranchers and natives fought over grazing lands and hunting rights, smugglers from the United States brought whiskey across the border, and prospectors and outlaws gathered in ramshackle towns without police officers, or even laws. Sam believed that a force of 1,000 trained men would be necessary to bring order to the Prairies. He was sent with 250 recruits.

Even getting to the western territories was no easy task. The horses stampeded during a thunder storm and had to be rounded up, the men ran out of feed for the animals, and the travellers sometimes waded through mud up to their knees.

At one point, Sam was helping round up some cattle when he and his horse jumped a small stream and sank up to their necks in quicksand. Quickly lying flat on his belly and "swimming" toward firmer ground, Sam gently coaxed his horse after him until the animal was free.

Sam described one part of the march like this:

> *The trail was worse than any we had encountered. It was knee-deep in black mud, sloughs crossed it every few hundred yards, and the wagons had to be unloaded and dragged through them by hand. Many small ponds covered with a thin coating of ice lined*

FAST FACT

Sam's life wasn't all gunfights and blizzards. He wrote about plenty of parties and dances during his time in the West. In Fort McLeod, he met a 29-year-old woman named Marie Elizabeth Harwood. The couple married on January 15, 1890, and spent part of their honeymoon in New York City.

the sides of the trail . . . The poor animals, crazed with thirst and feverish because of their privations, would rush to the ponds to drink, often falling and having to be dragged out with ropes from when they fell.

As he travelled through this untamed territory, Sam gained a reputation as one of the toughest men in the country. He survived shootouts with whiskey traders and rode through blinding blizzards. He even held back rioting railway workers with a single shotgun while a young deputy stood beside him and shouted out the Riot Act.

According to one story, Sam caught Rocky Mountain spotted fever in 1879. As his temperature climbed and he grew delirious, his doctors were convinced that he would die during the night. A young officer volunteered to stay in his room. In the middle of the night, Sam awoke to find the officer lying on his floor. When he heard that the young man was expecting him to die at any moment, Sam said, "Go back to bed and let me get some rest." He soon recovered and returned to work.

Sam was also known as a fair man, one who enforced the law equally among white settlers and native people. He earned the respect of both the

BOYS AROUND THE WORLD

History is full of teenage con artists as well as teenage heroes. In the 1960s, 16-year-old Frank Abagnale Jr. began cashing forged cheques at a series of banks, stealing thousands of dollars. He went on to successfully pose as a pilot, a pediatrician, and a university professor. He was finally arrested in France in 1969. When he was released from prison, he opened his own consulting company to teach banks how to detect fraud.

government and the native chiefs of the Rocky Mountains and served as a mediator during land-claims negotiations.

In 1898, as prospectors flocked toward rumours of a gold rush in the Yukon, Sam was posted to the north. There, he set up a base at the border of Canadian territory, keeping order among the gold-seekers and sending criminals back across the Alaskan boundary. His reputation as a tough and fair officer had followed him north. Sam guarded a bank manager's stash of $2 million for an entire winter, without a locked safe, and no one attempted to break into his headquarters.

Sam spent more than a year almost single-handedly creating order in the Yukon before returning to Vancouver, then Montreal. Amazingly, he was still ready for adventure. He commanded a cavalry unit in the Boer War in South Africa. Then, at the age of 63, he was given command of 25,000 men in World War I.

Sam had just retired in 1918 when he was struck by influenza. He died in London, England, in 1919, a larger-than-life legend of the Canadian West.

HENRY FUNG

SPECIAL AGENT
1926–2003

The roar of the engines and the screaming wind almost deafened Henry as he leaned out the door of the Royal Air Force Liberator plane. It was the night of June 22, 1945, and so dark that he could barely see the ground far below. As he waited for the signal to jump, Henry felt as if his entire body were quivering with excitement. He was 19, and he was about to take a flying leap—literally—into the first battlefield of his life.

For most of World War II, Chinese-Canadians had been excluded from the war effort. Racism was still rampant in Canada (Chinese immigrants were not even allowed to vote), and the government worried that Asian-Canadians who enlisted as soldiers might become spies for the Japanese.

Then, in 1943 and 1944, the British approached the Canadian government with a special request. They needed young, fit, Chinese-Canadian men to become spies for the British in the jungles of Asia.

Hundreds of Chinese-Canadians volunteered, seeking adventure and eager to prove their loyalty to their new country. They were sent to training camps in Canada, Australia, and India. Assigned to a base in Calcutta, India, Henry found himself studying jungle fighting methods, map-reading, and bombs and other weapons. Most of his fellow recruits never made it to the front lines before the war ended. But Henry was one of the few who did.

After his leap from the plane, he landed in a jungle clearing deep in Malaya, where guerilla fighters were waging a violent war against the Japanese army, which had occupied their country. As he extricated himself from his parachute, already sweating in the humid warmth of the jungle, Henry met his new partners—soldiers with the Malayan People's Anti-Japanese Army (MPAJA), the rebel fighters he had come to help.

BOYS AROUND THE WORLD

Thirteen-year-old John Condon used his older brother's identification to enlist in the British army during World War I. He was killed in a battle at Ypres, Belgium, five months later—the youngest Allied soldier to die in the war.

Most of the guerillas were young, with no previous battle experience and no formal training. They had become soldiers simply because they were dedicated to forcing the Japanese out of Malaya. Still, Henry had to admit that they knew their way around the jungle. For four days and four nights, he and the other agents who had parachuted with him followed the guerillas down trails, across roads, and through swamps until they reached a hidden camp south of Kuala Lumpur (now the capital city of Malaysia).

Once the special agents had arranged themselves in the jungle camp, they radioed the British forces. Soon, planes flew low overhead to drop weapons, food, equipment, and medicine for the agents and the guerillas.

Henry and his team set about training the guerilla fighters and making life as difficult as possible for the Japanese army. Moving along hidden jungle trails, often at night, they managed to plant explosives at the base of a vital railway bridge and destroy the bridge and the surrounding tracks. They sabotaged telephone lines, leaving the Japanese unable to communicate between cities. They ambushed supply trucks, trying to deprive the army of as much food and equipment as possible.

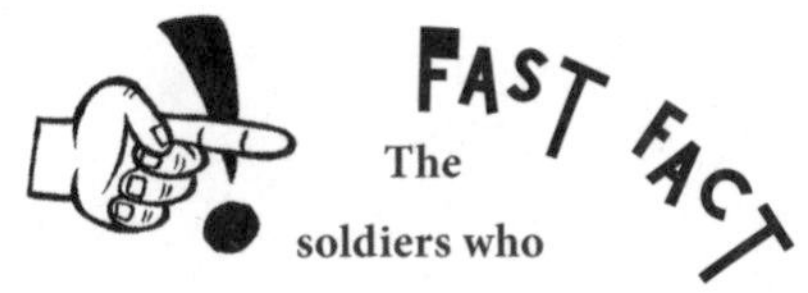

The soldiers who served in the jungles of Malaya soon learned that there were three things almost as daunting as Japanese soldiers—monsoons, mosquitoes, and malaria. Luckily, Henry managed to escape malaria. The other two were harder to avoid.

When the Japanese finally surrendered at the end of World War II, Henry and his team were sent to the city of Kajang, where they were supposed to take control of the military base. But when they arrived, the Japanese soldiers wouldn't come out. They were afraid that they would be beaten or killed by the MPAJA guerillas. So the team waited for British reinforcements to arrive.

After that, Henry was off to Kuala Lumpur to help organize prisoners of war. Eventually he flew back home to Vancouver, British Columbia.

When the war ended, British Columbia awarded all Chinese-Canadian veterans the right to vote in future provincial elections. Soon after, the rest of Canada followed. Henry Fung not only succeeded in his mission to help the world, he started changes in his own country as well.

HOW WILL YOU ROCK THE WORLD?

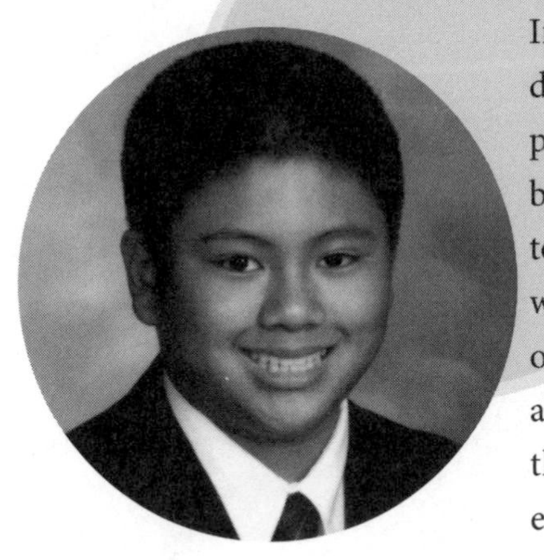

If I achieved my wildest dream of becoming an NBA player, I'd rock the world by being the first Chinese-Canadian to have made it to the league. I would help promote the game all over the world and talk to people about basketball. It's my dream for the NBA to one day have teams on every single continent on earth.

— Jacob, age 13

BRAINIACS

ROCKING THE INTELLECTUAL WORLD

Sandford Fleming

Inventor and Engineer

1827–1915

Sandford Fleming was an 18-year-old novice engineer when he left his Scotland home onboard the Brilliant, a cargo ship headed for Canada. Two weeks later, as a storm hammered the vessel, he sealed this letter in a bottle and tossed it into the waves:

> *Dear Father . . . end of April, 1845, on board ship Brilliant. We have come through a three days gale from the northwest. Blown several hundred miles south of our course. Wind has stopped, but sea is worse than ever. Iron bars in cargo broken loose in the hold. Ship not expected to last much longer. We send love to all. God keep you.*

Contrary to their expectations, Sandford and his brother managed to survive the voyage. A month after leaving Scotland, they disembarked in Quebec City and set off on a journey to Upper Canada.

Soon, Sandford had a job in Peterborough, drafting maps of the new country around him. Finding no one to print his finished maps, he invested in some equipment and began producing and selling maps of the surrounding cities. Around this time, the young man also came up with his first invention—an in-line skate.

Eager to get out of the office and explore more of Canada, Sandford trained as a land surveyor. He also founded the Canadian Institute, a kind of club where academics and scientists could discuss new ideas. But after a few monthly meetings, only Sandford and one other man were still showing up. Determined not to give up on his plan, Sandford decided that the society would have to meet more often, not less. He sent out a letter to all the members, and his club was soon growing. (Now known as the Royal Canadian Institute, the society has about 800 members and hosts public lectures at the University of Toronto.)

BOYS AROUND THE WORLD

Blaise Pascal, a child prodigy and mathematical genius, was born in France in 1623. By the time he was 16, he was developing his own mathematical theories, as well as something more recognizable to the rest of us—the mechanical adding machine, precursor to the calculator.

He embarked on a variety of work projects, from creating Canada's first postage stamp to charting the Toronto harbour and designing Peterborough's cemetery. But one of Sandford's most cherished ideas was a coast-to-coast railway linking all of Canada. He accepted a job planning tracks from the Maritimes to Quebec. Then, in 1872, he was hired by the Canadian government to survey a route to the Pacific Ocean. Thirteen years later, he was present when Donald Smith drove in the famous "last spike" of the continental railway.

Trains brought with them a new problem—schedules. In every city and town in North America, people set the time using the sun as a guide. But because the sun peaked at varying times, every city's time might be slightly different. For example, noon in Ottawa might have been considered 12:15 in Sudbury. After missing one too many trains because of misprinted information or time confusion, Sandford came up with a startling plan. He suggested that the entire world base its time on one 24-hour clock, using Greenwich, England, as the base. (England already based all its clocks on Greenwich time.) Radiating out from Greenwich,

FAST FACT

Sandford's panicked message-in-a-bottle was found seven months after the storm by a fisher in Devon, England. Luckily, the Fleming family in Scotland received it after Sandford had already written home about finding a job in Peterborough, Ontario.

local time zones would be adjusted for each region.

After discussing the idea at length with the members of the Canadian Institute, Sandford began to promote it at international conferences. By the end of the 1920s, nations around the world had changed their clocks. Sandford became known as the inventor of standard time.

In his later years, Sandford spearheaded a movement to link the entire British Empire by telegraph. He was knighted by Queen Victoria in 1897 and died in 1915.

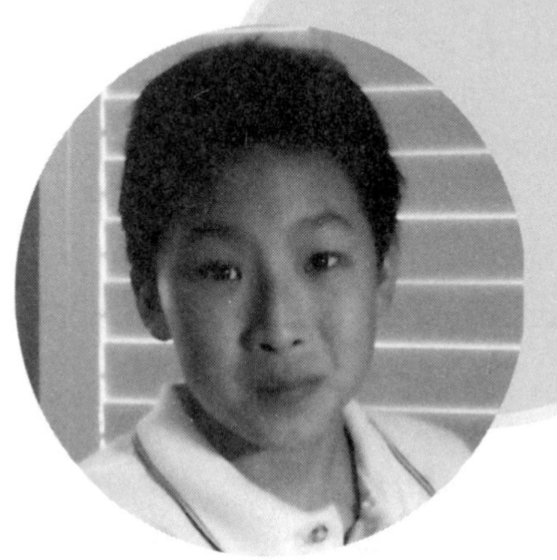

HOW WILL YOU ROCK THE WORLD?

If I could rock the world,
I would create a watch
where you would put in a destination and be transported there right away. This will help you in traffic situations and going somewhere when you're too tired to move.

— *Aaron, age 12*

MARK BLUVSHTEIN

INTERNATIONAL GRANDMASTER

1988–

Row after row of blue, cloth-draped tables extended across the massive conference centre like parallel rivers. And in each row floated countless chessboards.

Competitors sat almost elbow-to-elbow. One was clutching her hair; another stared blankly ahead, mentally picturing his next move. Amid the hushed chaos, Mark Bluvshtein folded his arms across his chest and focused on the board. He didn't hear the whispered conversations nearby, or the footsteps of the official walking the aisle, or the snap of the press photographers' shutters. His world had narrowed to include only the black and white pieces in front of him. He had controlled the opening of the game, but there was no way to predict exactly what his opponent would do, or when. To Mark, chess was a mental battle and victory lay in achieving absolute perfection.

Born in the USSR, Mark moved to Israel with his parents and older sister when he was five years old. Six years after that, the family settled permanently in Toronto, Canada.

Shortly after arriving in Israel, Mark began playing regular chess games with his dad. By the time he was six, he was studying with private coaches

Boys Around the World

Born in 1888, Cuban chess prodigy José Raúl Capablanca learned to play the game when he was four years old, and won a match with Cuba's most famous player when he was only 13. He was the world chess champion from 1921 to 1927.

and competing in chess competitions. According to his dad, the young boy's talent was immediately obvious. And when Mark beat an International Master at the age of 11, he began to draw attention from serious chess fans.

Even in elementary school, Mark was already one of Canada's best chess players, with invitations to tournaments around the world. When he was 13, the World Chess Federation awarded him the title of International Master. He was the youngest Canadian International Master in history.

Three years later, he broke more age records to become the youngest-ever International Grandmaster. By that time, Mark had met and matched wits with chess geniuses from North America, Europe, and Asia. He had competed for Canada in two World Youth Chess Championships, and he had been named Canadian chess player of the year for two years in a row. In 2005, he was the Canadian champion in his age group, and tied for third place in the world championships for players under 18.

Fast Fact

Mark speaks three languages: English, Hebrew, and Russian.

Although he dedicates about 20 hours a week to chess, Mark tries to balance his study time with time for basketball, soccer, tennis, and his family and friends. At the same time, he relishes the opportunity to see the world, and looks forward to more international competitions in the future.

JOHN TUZO WILSON

GEOPHYSICIST
1908–1993

John Tuzo Wilson stopped one of his fellow geophysicists in the hallway at Cambridge University.

"I have discovered a new class of fault," he said.

The professor looked at him skeptically. John had been researching the movements of the earth's crust for years now, and many scientists thought his ideas were ridiculous. After all, how could the entire crust of the earth move?

Seeing that his colleague was doubtful, John whipped a piece of folded construction paper out of his wallet. By pushing the folded paper together, then pulling it apart, he demonstrated how two plates, floating on a layer of molten rock, could move against one another.

All of a sudden, the skeptical professor felt as if he were seeing something completely new and original. He examined the model closely, then looked at John again. This, he decided, was a very clever man.

John had been excelling in school since the primary grades, but he had always thought of geology as more fun than work. When he was 15, his father arranged a summer job for him in a forestry camp. Two years after that, he became a field assistant to Noel Odell, a geologist and mountaineer who had once climbed Everest. Noel intro-duced the teenager to the mysteries of the rock beneath his feet.

FAST FACT

In the Valley of the Ten Peaks in Alberta's Rocky Mountains looms an imposing summit named Mount Tuzo. It's named not for John, but for his mother. Henrietta Tuzo was the first person ever to climb the mountain. She met John's father at a camp organized by the Alpine Club of Canada.

At the time, there were countless unanswered questions in geology. No one knew how the continents had formed or why volcanoes erupted. Because of these gaps in knowledge, many physicists and chemists thought of geology as an amateur science, all about collecting rocks, certainly nothing that would advance people's understanding of the world.

That's why John's instructors were shocked when after one year as a physics student at the University of Toronto, John decided he wanted to pursue geology as well. This young man has a brilliant physics career ahead of him, they thought. Why would he waste his intelligence peering at cliffs and craters? And John couldn't really explain his interest. After all, he knew only a handful of scientists working in the field—two studying earthquakes, one studying gravity, a handful investigating the earth's magnetic field, and a few more looking for valuable minerals.

Undeterred by the lack of support, John managed to convince a professor to create two courses in geophysics. (In one of them, John was the only student!) He graduated in 1930, the first Canadian-trained geophysicist. John went on to study at Cambridge University, then Princeton, earning his doctorate in 1936.

John's early years in the field were filled with adventure as well as research. After World War II, when he discovered that Canada had a collection of army vehicles sitting unused in the Arctic, he organized history's only vehicle journey across the Arctic. With a group of researchers, he travelled for 5,500 kilometres (3,400 miles) from Churchill, Manitoba, to the northern ice pack. Along the way, one of his team members confirmed the location of the magnetic North Pole.

John went on to map Canada's glaciers, study the formation of mountains, and finally investigate continental drift. The theory that the earth's crust "drifted" over a layer of molten rock had been proposed by a German scientist in 1912. But no one believed him. In fact, until the 1960s, anyone who believed in continental drift was considered a crackpot.

FAST FACT

The San Andreas Fault off the southern coast of California (the same fault line involved in the San Francisco-area earthquakes) is a transform fault, like the one that John described to his colleague using a construction paper model.

But in 1959, new research was published that supported the theory, and John became a convert. The idea seemed to answer all sorts of questions about canyons, volcanoes, and earthquakes. When he flew over the Hawaiian islands, for example, he could see that volcanoes there must be caused by a "hot spot" under the earth's crust.

For the next decade, John tried to convince his fellow scientists that the theory was correct. He wrote more than 60 articles and spoke in a famous debate. And gradually, his colleagues began to believe him. Soon, John was winning medals and trophies for his work. He was inducted to the Order of Canada in 1969.

John retired as a professor in 1974, but he immediately accepted another full-time job at the Ontario Science Centre. There, between paperwork, a gruelling travel schedule, and endless meetings, the 70-year-old scientist could be found playing video games with visiting school groups.

BOYS AROUND THE WORLD

History's most famous physicist is Albert Einstein, the German-born genius who discovered the relationships between light, gravity, and time. Born in 1879, Einstein published his first scientific research in 1894. He went on to win the Nobel Prize for Physics in 1921.

HUGH LE CAINE

MUSICIAN AND PHYSICIST

1914–1977

Ten-year-old Hugh Le Caine had been scampering around the community hall in Port Arthur, Ontario, when he heard raised voices. He crept closer to listen. His mother and the rest of the cast of the community play were standing frozen as the pianist argued with one of the directors.

Hugh didn't understand what they were arguing about, and he didn't understand why everyone was so upset when the frustrated pianist gathered up his music sheets and stormed out of the theatre.

"He took all the music with him," Hugh's mother explained to him. "We won't be able to do the show."

Hugh still didn't see the problem. After all, he'd been hearing that music for weeks. He had memorized every single note.

Hugh had been surrounded by music since birth. A piano, violin, guitar, and autoharp all held places in his home. When he was four years old, he noticed a nail sticking out of a scrap piece of wood near his house. He discovered that by hitting the nail with another nail, he could make a ringing sound. Soon, he had borrowed his father's hammer to create his own instrument by banging more nails into a board.

By the time he was six, he was playing the piano to accompany his sister's singing performances. And by high school, Hugh had developed a keen interest in both music and science. He was experimenting with complicated sounds by holding a microphone in front of his dad's radio speaker to create feedback. Around the same time, he build an electronics workshop in his bedroom where he could conduct tests with electricity.

Hugh was always experimenting. He would be struck by the amazing possibilities of a new idea—an electric ukulele, perhaps—and dedicate all his energy for weeks into perfecting the instrument. Then reality would set in and he would conclude that the instrument was useless, or the sound was wrong, or the parts he needed were unattainable. He would stomp around the house feeling depressed . . . until another idea dawned.

Hugh enrolled at Queen's University in 1934, and began a long career in physics. He completed a master's degree, earned a research fellowship, and worked on devices to measure radiation and vibration. During World War II, he was a member of a team that helped develop some of the first radar systems.

Along with his physics-related work, Hugh was still pursuing his first passion—music. He studied with an acclaimed piano teacher, scrutinized newly created instruments, and continued to work on his own inventions. In 1937, he began work on an electronic organ—his first successful electronic instrument.

The most famous instrument Hugh invented was the sackbut. Today, the name is unfamiliar, but the instrument itself is played by both children and professional musicians. The sackbut was the world's first synthesizer. Instead of using strings or reeds, it created sound by using electricity to vibrate the diaphragms of a speaker. And by including touch-sensitive keys and easily adjusted dials, Hugh created the first electronic instrument that could be used by ordinary people.

Hugh composed and performed several pieces of music to demonstrate the advantages of his electronic organ and sackbut. When his public demonstrations proved successful, he was offered a job by the National Research Council. There, he was able to set up his own laboratory and dedicate himself to creating new ways to make music. He happily gave up his career in physics and invented 22 musical instruments over the next 20 years.

As the popularity of his instruments grew, and as other inventors and musicians across the continent began to experiment, electronic music slowly gained acceptance. By the 1950s, universities were even starting to ponder starting their own electronic music programs. Hugh helped the University of Toronto create a studio in 1959. McGill University built one in 1964.

FAST FACT

Hugh loved trick photography. He once cut out a picture of himself, propped it up in his flower bed, and took a close-up photograph. When he developed the second photo, it looked like he was standing amid giant garden flowers.

Hugh was just as eccentric as he was successful. For example, he believed that he worked best during the first four hours of his day. After that, his mind was tired and his productivity levels slowed. He decided to rearrange his days, working for four hours, then taking four hours of personal time, then sleeping for four hours. He still worked eight hours a day, but not necessarily at the same times as his co-workers did.

Hugh had always believed that his life of inventing took up too much time for him to marry or raise a family. Instead, he spent his free time with friends or riding his motorcycle. But in 1959, a high school teacher named Trudi Janowski convinced him that he had been wrong. They were married at Toronto City Hall in 1960. Even though she hadn't realized what a strange schedule Hugh followed, Trudi managed to continue her teaching job

BOYS AROUND THE WORLD

Charles Wheatstone had his first musical composition published in Britain when he was 15. Like Hugh, he was also a noted scientist who helped to develop the telegraph and invented an early microphone. In 1829, he invented a form of accordion.

and have dinner with her husband at midnight each night, when he was finished his most productive hours of work.

Though his inventions became famous, Hugh was never completely comfortable in public. His friends said that sometimes he would happily attend parties and offer performances, but at other times he would retreat to the quiet of his own home. He also never regarded himself as a great musician. The compositions he wrote to showcase the potential of his instruments are now recognized as some of the first great contributions to electronic music. But when Hugh was asked why one of his pieces was called "Dripsody," he said it was written by a drip.

Hugh died in 1977 after a motorcycle accident.

?

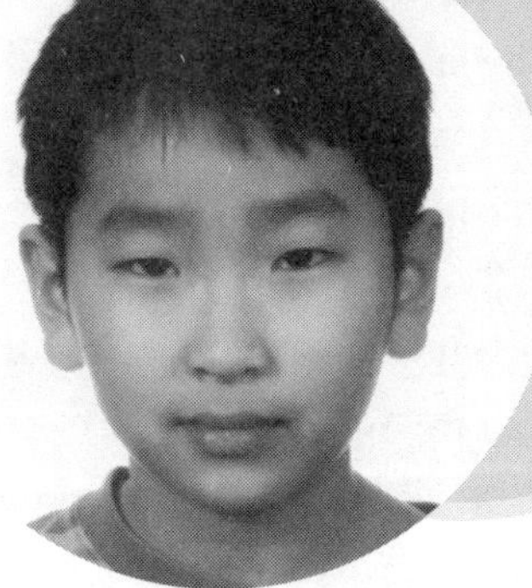

I will find a new way to do math, so people will be smarter.

— Ryan, age 8

HOW WILL YOU ROCK THE WORLD?

If I could rock the world I would invent a car that uses carbon monoxide as fuel and changes it back to oxygen. I would do this because even if you were going to be lazy and drive, it would still be clean, like biking.

— Matthew, age 13

REGINALD FESSENDEN

INVENTOR
1866–1932

Tren Fessenden kneeled at the banks of the river and banged two rocks together below the surface. The length of a football field away, his older brother Reginald plunged his entire head into the chilly water, and listened. There . . . he heard it. Above the gurgling of the water itself, he could hear the banging rocks.

Pleased with their experiment, the boys "borrowed" two of their mother's pots, pounded holes in the bottom, and connected them with string. Reginald shouted into a pot while Tren pressed his ear to the second. Sure enough, he could hear his brother's voice.

But Reginald wasn't satisfied. He knew that even as they played, inventor Alexander Graham Bell was experimenting with sending a voice through a wire using electricity. Reginald had no idea how it was done, but he was determined to find out.

Born in East Bolton, Quebec, Reginald moved to Ontario with his family when still a young boy, partly after his missed classes and practical jokes led his minister father to believe that Reginald should be enrolled in military school. One of the youngest students at his new academy, he was a quick learner. He easily made the honour roll, and went on to become a boarder at a school in Port Hope.

Reginald found most of his classes too easy to hold his attention. Instead, he devoted himself to keeping up with the successes of his inventor hero. Reginald's Uncle Cortez was actually present at some of Alexander Graham Bell's experiments and fascinated the young boy with stories of voices travelling through wires into a receiver in a nearby building.

Reginald was so enthralled by science that he would stay up half the night reading his father's textbooks. His mother began locking the study and sleeping with the key around her neck, just to make sure that her son got enough sleep. Secretly, Reginald stole the key, made a copy, and returned the original, so he could continue his midnight readings.

By the time he was 14, Reginald had absorbed all he could at the boarding school and had earned a scholarship to Bishop's College in Quebec. Four years later, he accepted a job as headmaster at a school in Bermuda. But Reginald worried about missing out on new research happening in the scientific community. In his 20s, he trained as an electrician and returned to the United States, pestering the famous inventor Thomas Edison and hanging around his work crews. Eventually, one of the workers quit unexpectedly. Reginald leaped at the opportunity and joined Edison's team, creating insulation for electrical wires. When he took an extra job insulating wires for a rich homeowner nearby, Reginald earned enough money for a down payment on an engagement ring for a woman he'd met in Bermuda. And not long after, he began teaching electrical engineering at an American university.

FAST FACT

Other inventors such as Guglielmo Marconi were trying to transmit radio broadcasts in short bursts of electricity. But Reginald believed that the waves must radiate out from an antenna, like ripples radiate from a pebble dropped in a pond. Time proved him right, and the first radio transmissions of voice used his "continuous waves."

Throughout his early days working for the inventor, Reginald kept dreaming of ways to transmit human voices—not through telephone wires like Alexander Graham Bell but through the air without any wires at all. Most people thought his ideas were ludicrous, but in 1900 he got a job with the United States Weather Bureau, where he was given the time and resources to work on his own inventions. He had soon perfected his most innovative idea yet—an early version of a radio receiver.

On Christmas Eve that same year, Reginald embarked on an ambitious experiment. He asked workers at his company to listen for a transmission, then he prepared his equipment in a small hut near the Potomac River. That evening, he successfully sent his own words through a wireless telephone, achieving history's first radio transmission of a human voice. He played "O, Holy Night" on his violin, read the Christmas story, and wished a Merry Christmas to all his listeners.

Over the next decade, Reginald continued to work on ways to transmit voices and Morse code without wires. He devised new receivers, designed a system to allow submarines to signal each other, and created a device that could detect icebergs while they were still far away from approaching ships.

Reginald died at his vacation home in Bermuda in 1932. By that time, he held more than 500 patents for inventions—more than any other man except Thomas Edison. Although not many Canadians know of him today, people who work in radio remember Reginald as the father of radio broadcasting.

BOYS AROUND THE WORLD

Born in 1809, Louis Braille spent many of his young years in a harsh school for visually impaired boys in Paris, France. When he was 12, the talented cello and organ player met a former soldier who showed him how the army used raised dots as a code that could be read at night. Louis spent the next three years perfecting a simpler system of raised dots that would allow blind people to read. His system is now used around the world.

TRAIL BLAZERS

ROCKING NEW FRONTIERS

HENRY KELSEY

EXPLORER
1667–1724

Henry Kelsey and a native guide were hiking along a river near Hudson Bay when they rounded a corner and stumbled upon two grizzly bears. Panicking, the guide leapt into a nearby evergreen, while Henry scrambled into a clump of willows. One of the bears charged the evergreen, but Henry fired his rifle and sent the bear crashing to the ground. The second bear charged toward the clump of willows. Luckily, Henry was well hidden, and the animal wasn't able to pick him out amid the branches. As the bear turned back to the man in the evergreen, Henry fired again.

Among the traders at the Hudson's Bay Company fort in what is now northern Manitoba, the wiry young man was known as "Boy Kelsey." But along the trading routes of the north, Henry became famous as the "Little Giant," the one who felled two grizzly bears.

Henry was born in England in 1667 and became an apprentice to the Hudson's Bay Company when he was 14. He embarked on a sea journey to a completely unknown and unmapped northern region of Canada. When he arrived at the fort, his duties included sorting and counting beaver pelts, gathering and chopping wood, feeding the fires, and hunting.

The Hudson's Bay Company had been trading with native groups along the shores of Hudson Bay for almost two decades, but no one had dared to follow the rivers inland and explore the unmapped areas of the country. To many of the men working at the fort, the harsh weather and wild animals of the region were terrifying. And they had good reason to be scared—Henry once found the bones and bloody clothes of a trader who had been eaten by wolves.

Henry was undaunted by the hard work at the fort and soon made friends with both the English and the native traders. When he was 21, he earned a chance to prove himself. Messengers had been sent to another company post far down the coast and had never returned. Kelsey cheerfully set out with a native guide and travelled for a month to deliver the messages successfully.

A year later, he set off again to make contact with native groups to the north and help establish trading relationships. He walked through swamps, clouds of mosquitoes, and constant rainstorms for more than 480 kilometres (300 miles). Along the way, he became the first white man to travel by land across northern Manitoba and the first to see an animal new to white people—the musk ox.

But Henry wasn't satisfied with his accomplishments. In 1690, he seized a chance to travel to the interior with a group of native traders. He embarked with supplies for a year of trading, gift-giving, and peace-making: guns, gunpowder, tobacco, a brass kettle, beads, hatchets, and a peace pipe. Along his journey, he would meet with as many native groups as possible, showing them the goods that the Hudson's Bay Company could offer and encouraging traders to take their furs north to the fort.

His mission was far from easy. At times, his group travelled for days with only a

BOYS AROUND THE WORLD

Historians believe that Norse explorer Leif Ericson was 20 when he bought a boat and set sail for North America in the year 1000. He was probably the first non-First Nations person to see Baffin Island and Newfoundland.

few birds for food. At other times, bad weather or low water levels forced them to leave their canoes and slog overland. Despite the hardships, Henry spent two years exploring and managed to see much of what is now Manitoba and Saskatchewan, including the grasslands of the prairie, the massive buffalo herds, and the legendary grizzly bears.

Henry had made extraordinary discoveries and had convinced more native traders to do business with the Hudson's Bay Company. But the company didn't publicize his achievements. Henry's supervisors considered his explorations private company business and didn't want to draw too much attention from their competitors. If not for Henry's own journals, he might not be recognized as the first European to travel the plains.

FAST FACT

After Henry returned to Hudson Bay, the fort was temporarily captured by the French. He was forced to spend the winter fending for himself in the woods and was one of only 25 men to survive. Eighteen others were killed by hunger, exposure, and disease.

HOW WILL YOU ROCK THE WORLD?

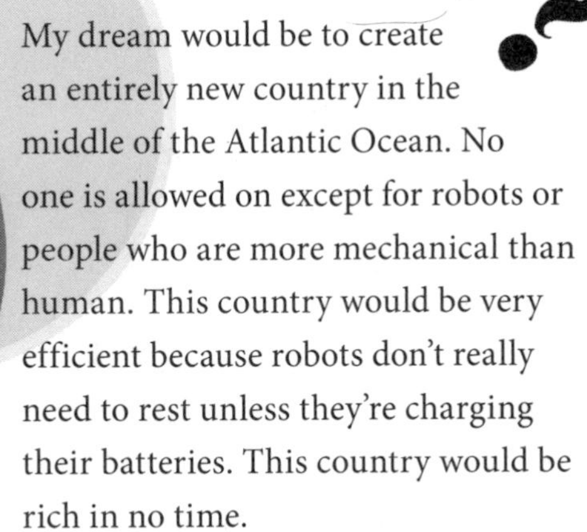

My dream would be to create an entirely new country in the middle of the Atlantic Ocean. No one is allowed on except for robots or people who are more mechanical than human. This country would be very efficient because robots don't really need to rest unless they're charging their batteries. This country would be rich in no time.

— *Hadrian, age 13*

SIMON JACKSON

ACTIVIST
1982-

Watching the television news with his family one night, seven-year-old Simon Jackson saw a story about the threatened habitat of Kodiak bears in Alaska. The majestic-looking brown bears caught the young boy's interest. According to the story, there were only a few thousand of the animals in the entire world. How could loggers or developers risk their extinction?

Simon thought back to the family of grizzlies he'd seen while on a summer vacation in Yellowstone National Park. The massive mother bear had led her two cubs across a meadow near the road. The size and strength of the mother and the playfulness of the cubs had impressed Simon, and he'd never forgotten them.

Clearly, Simon couldn't sit idle. He opened a lemonade stand near his home on Vancouver's North Shore and raised $60 for the cause. He also wrote to the prime minister of Canada and the president of the United States. Just a few months later, he received a letter about the preservation of the Kodiak's habitat. His letters had helped!

When he was 13, Simon learned about the threatened rainforest habitat of another type of bear. The white kermode, or spirit bear, lived along the coast of northern British Columbia. Because of a recessive gene, one out of every 10 black bears was born with white fur—making the white bears a genetically unique subspecies. According to native legend, the distinctive coat was a reminder that the lush rainforest had once been a pristine land of ice and snow.

When Simon learned about the spirit bear, logging and hunting were forcing the creatures to the edge of extinction—less than 400 of them remained. He discovered that the spirit bear was just as unique to British Columbia as the panda was to China, yet hardly anyone had heard of it. Determined to change that, he embarked on a campaign, speaking to every English class in his school and collecting 700 letters to send to the British Columbia premier.

Next, Simon founded the Spirit Bear Youth Coalition, an organization run entirely by youth and dedicated to saving the rainforest habitat. For the rest of his high school years, he campaigned to have the voices of the youth taken seriously, to educate the public about the plight of the spirit bear, and to find solutions that helped preserve both the forest and the province's economy.

As Simon's movement grew, he found help from thousands of young people around the world, as well as from several celebrities. J.K. Rowling, Dr. Jane Good-all, and the rock bands Nickelback and the Backstreet Boys pledged their support. Even Prince William joined the cause after Simon stood among hundreds of teenage girls and waved a spirit bear book until he caught the prince's attention.

BOYS AROUND THE WORLD

Olaudah Equino was captured by slavers in Africa in 1756, when he was 11 years old. After a horrific sea voyage and forced labour in the West Indies, he was bought by the captain of a trading ship. On board, he learned to read and write. Eventually, Olaudah wrote an autobiography that exposed the intolerable working conditions and extreme violence faced by slaves. Published in English, Dutch, and German, the book helped spark movements to abolish slavery. The Atlantic slave trade was finally stopped 10 years after Olaudah's death.

By 2000, the Spirit Bear Youth Coalition had become an international organization, and *Time* magazine named Simon one of "60 Heroes for the Planet." Suddenly, Simon was famous. He gave hundreds of interviews to television, radio, and newspaper journalists. And in 2001, as the government worked on a new land-use plan for the spirit bear habitat, 25,000 letters flooded the premier's office.

FAST FACT

The spirit bear lives 500 kilometres (310 miles) north of Vancouver. Its rainforest habitat is also home to salmon, deer, wolves, and grizzlies. In 2006, the spirit bear was named British Columbia's provincial animal.

Today, Simon's organization has grown to become the largest youth-led initiative in the world, with a network of more than six million in more than 60 countries around the world. With two-thirds of the spirit bear's home now saved, his Youth Coalition continues to work to protect the final unprotected habitat. In one of their newest ventures, they're producing an animated movie with the same team that made *The Lion King*. When *The Spirit Bear* is released, a portion of the profits will go directly toward helping save the bear. As logging companies fight for access to the northern forests, the coalition continues to serve as the voice of the spirit bear.

Meanwhile, Simon is serving as the executive producer of the movie, working toward a university degree, and travelling the world to speak about habitat protection. Now that he's had an up-close look at how powerful young people can be, he hopes to work with youth on other causes in the future.

JOSEPH ELZÉAR BERNIER

EXPLORER
1852–1934

Joseph Elzéar Bernier watched the last shadows of the Canadian coastline disappear over the horizon and felt a shiver of excitement. This was hardly his first sea voyage. In fact, Joseph had sailed from Canada to Cuba when he was only two years old, on board one of his father's ships. But this voyage was different. Now, he was master of the ship. He was 17 years old, an official sea captain, and on his way across the Atlantic.

Joseph was born in 1852 in L'Islet, Quebec, and had spent his life among sailors and captains, explorers and traders. When he made his trans-Atlantic voyage at 17 and successfully brought back a shipload of wood from Ireland, he embarked on a lifetime of travel. In total, he would make more than 100 voyages.

But it was a stop along the east coast of the United States that would change Joseph's life. While docked on the Potomac River in 1871, he saw the *Polaris* being outfitted for a trip to the North Pole. Heavy iron and oak beams were being added to the hull, to help the ship withstand the pressure of the ice as it spent a season locked in the Arctic sea. Meanwhile, the ship's captain was gathering supplies for life in the north: cold-weather gear, ample food, sleds, and sled dogs.

To Joseph, the entire enterprise seemed to have sprung from the pages of an adventure story. He began collecting all the material he could find about the Arctic, reading the accounts of past explorers, whalers, and scientists. Soon, he was writing proposals for northern journeys. He was convinced that if he sailed to the ocean north of Siberia and allowed his ship to be locked in the ice, the currents would carry him within reach of the pole. In 1904, he even purchased a ship for the voyage, naming it the *Arctic*.

At first, the Canadian government was supportive. But at the last moment, officials asked Joseph to abandon his polar expedition and carry a contingent of police officers north to catch a criminal and to establish police posts on some of the islands.

When he returned, still hoping to arrange a voyage to the pole, the government had new concerns. A Norwegian explorer had charted Ellesmere Island and was pressuring the Norwegian government to claim the land. At the same time, the United States government was looking for a northern island where it could build an air base. It funded an expedition to survey several possibilities.

To the Canadian government, these were both alarming developments. Canada wanted control over its Arctic borders, and wasn't willing to cede Ellesmere Island to Norway, or to allow American planes to blithely fly in and out of Canadian airspace. After passing a law that required all Arctic explorers and scientists to carry a Canadian licence, the government sent Joseph to intercept the American mission.

So in 1910, Joseph again took the *Arctic* north and met the American scientists at a remote island outpost. Already plagued

FAST FACT

The *Polaris* voyage that inspired Joseph's interest in the Arctic ended in disaster. The captain died under mysterious circumstances, and 18 members of the crew were stranded on an ice floe for six months until a ship managed to rescue them.

by mechanical difficulties and bad weather, the Americans turned back and left the Arctic without choosing a location for their air base.

Joseph travelled to the north 12 times between 1906 and 1925, spending eight winters locked in the ice and even developing a new sport—baseball on the ice. To keep the crew occupied, Joseph staged the games on the pack ice outside the ship, even in –20°C (–4°F) weather.

BOYS AROUND THE WORLD

English explorer John Franklin went to sea when he was 14 and helped his uncle chart the coast of Australia just a few years later. In 1845, Franklin set off to find a northwest passage through the ice of northern Canada. The entire expedition disappeared. Fourteen years later, another explorer found a cairn and a journal describing how Franklin's ships had become locked in the ice for two seasons. The sailors had died of cold, starvation, and lead poisoning from their tinned food supplies.

During his voyages, the explorer tracked foreign whalers and fishers and issued them Canadian permits, mapped and claimed islands for Canada, and helped establish police posts. When he and the *Arctic* retired in 1925, Canada had established sovereignty over 740,000 square kilometres (285,700 square miles) of the north.

Kozo Shimotakahara

Doctor

1855–1951

Kozo Shimotakahara stood on the deck of the boat and looked back toward the beach of his hometown. It seemed as if his entire family, all his neighbours, and every friend he had ever made in Kagoshima, Japan, had gathered to wish him well. As dusk fell, they built bonfires on the sand, and even as Kozo's vessel steamed its way further down the coast, he could see the bright spots of orange glowing in the distance.

Fourteen-year-old Kozo wasn't the first one in his family to embark for North America. His brother had gone several years before, hoping to study medicine. But his brother had died of tuberculosis, and Kozo had decided to become a doctor in his place. So, with his mother's life savings of five yen—egg money—in his pockets, he left Japan behind forever.

Kozo was 15 when he arrived in Vancouver, British Columbia. In 1900, it was a bustling seaport full of loggers and sailors, prosperous business-people, and penniless new arrivals. Other immigrants directed Kozo to a dormitory run by a Japanese Methodist minister, where beds were set aside for people who arrived without family members or friends to support them. Kozo was the youngest person there.

Watching the trade going on in the streets around him, the young adventurer decided his first priority should be to learn English. He enrolled himself in the local elementary school, where he sat among six-year-olds until he could read and write. Four years later, he went on to Britannia High School. To support himself, he did chores for several elderly couples, earning barely enough to eat. Kozo was a short man, and for the rest of his life he would wonder if the shortage of food during his teenage years had hampered his growth forever.

Obviously, he was going to have to find a way to make more money. Travelling to nearby Steveston, Kozo signed on with a notoriously bad-tempered fisherman and spent the summer working especially hard and cooking his boss Japanese delicacies. By the end of the season, the fisherman was so impressed that he gave Kozo half of the season's profits—an unheard-of amount of pay for someone in Kozo's situation.

In 1908, Kozo graduated from high school. After eight years of supporting himself and studying far into the night by the light of coal lamps, he must have considered giving up his dream of medical school and taking a job with the farmers and fishers in Vancouver. But Kozo was determined. He began classes at a college in New Westminster, then earned a place at the University of Chicago medical school. He worked so hard in the evenings as a cook, a servant, and a waiter that he was well known for falling asleep in class. Still, he graduated in 1912.

After another stint working to earn money for a train ticket, Kozo returned to the Pacific coast. He stopped in Seattle to write exams for medical licences. While he was in the city, Kozo stopped by the house of a prominent Japanese-American doctor to introduce himself. He was impressed by the doctor, but even more impressed by his daughter. When he passed his exams (with first-class honours), he asked Shin Kusama to marry him.

After Shin worked in a local doctor's office for six months—as training for marrying an up-and-coming doctor—the two set off for a honeymoon in Victoria, BC. They returned to Vancouver with a total of $2.

While the couple boarded at Kozo's old dormitory, he set up a medical practice out of a small room in a local church, becoming the first

Japanese-Canadian doctor in Canada. It wasn't long before his makeshift office was overflowing. Kozo rented a downtown building and used it as both a house and a clinic.

Kozo had already earned a stellar reputation in Vancouver when a flu epidemic struck in 1918. Working with other community leaders, Kozo helped transform a local school into an emergency clinic. Soon, volunteer nurses and doctors were working around the clock to treat the sick.

More than a decade later, Kozo was in the public eye again as one of the organizers of a medical clinic for people who couldn't afford to pay for a doctor. But all of his work in the community seemed forgotten with the outbreak of World War II. When Japan bombed Pearl Harbor in the United States, officials in the Canadian government became convinced that Japanese-Canadian immigrants were a threat to national security. They could be spies, sending information back to Japan and helping to plot future attacks.

Although there was no evidence that anyone was helping the Japanese army, the government confiscated the property of Japanese-Canadians and sent them to camps in the interior of British Columbia, far from the cities along the coast. Kozo lost his property as well, and although he was owed $15,000 by his patients, he cancelled their debts and moved with 2,000 immigrants to Kaslo, in BC's West Kootenay region. There he received the ridiculously low salary of $100 a month to serve as their doctor.

Despite the injustice of the move, Kozo quickly made a place for himself in Kaslo. Soon, word of his skill spread. Instead of just treating Japanese-Canadians, he began treating people from the entire community.

Kozo eventually made Kaslo his permanent home, continuing to work tirelessly for his patients. When he refused to stop making house calls even after suffering a heart attack, his wife gave up trying to slow him down and started accompanying him on all his visits. On November 30, 1951, he performed surgery in the morning and worked in the clinic all afternoon. He returned home too

FAST FACT

Kozo had a daughter and two sons, one of whom followed his father into medicine.

Boys Around the World

As Charles (Ohiyesa) Eastman was growing up in the 1860s, he assumed he would become a Sioux warrior. But the world was changing, and at 15 he was enrolled in a missionary school. Charles eventually became one of America's first Native doctors but spent much of his time fighting for the preservation of traditional First Nations culture.

tired to eat, and died of another heart attack that night. The entire town of Kaslo mourned his death: all the stores on the main street closed on the day of his funeral, so that everyone in the community would be free to attend.

How Will You Rock the World?

I would be the first person ever to invent a cure for cancer. Why cancer, you ask? Cancer has taken three lives in my family, and it needs to be put down, fast. Cancer kills millions of people each year and I am the one to put an end to it.

— *Connor, age 13*

Clennell Dickins

Bush Pilot

1899–1995

In January 1929, Clennell "Punch" Dickins peered at the frozen scene below. Everything looked uniformly white—both the icy expanse of Great Slave Lake and the unvaried barrens surrounding the shores. Only the few buildings of Fort Resolution, Northwest Territories, marked the landscape. When the ice formed each year, Fort Resolution was left inaccessible by land or water, isolated from the rest of the country. But in the cargo hold of his bush plane, Punch was carrying history's first airmail for the outpost.

Having swooped low over the shore and picked out a suitable landing strip, Punch lowered the aircraft towards the ice. The skis touched, and the plane hurtled forward along the lake. Then a jolt, and another. The ice was much rougher than it had looked from the air, even to Punch's experienced eye. When his craft finally slid to a stop, the propeller and underbelly of the plane were chipped and damaged.

Punch delivered his shipment of mail, then joined his mechanic to scrape off the damaged pieces of the propeller, bend the blades back into shape, and patch up the plane's body with some spare pieces of pipe. They were soon on their way back to base, and Punch was already thinking of his next flight. This time, he would carry the mail all the way to Aklavik, inside the Arctic Circle.

*

Punch had been gaining fame as one of Canada's top pilots since he was 18 years old. After joining the Royal Flying Corps, he trained as a pilot and swooped over the battlefields of World War I, completing 73 missions. He won the Distinguished Flying Cross for his success under fire.

But Punch's years in battle gave him more than a trophy. By the end of the war, he had practised under the most stressful conditions possible—dodging bullets, outmanoeuvering enemy planes, and deciphering complex maps and charts. He had also gained a thirst for adventure and a love of flying. He couldn't imagine doing anything else.

So, when he left the Air Force in 1927, Punch signed up with Western Canadian Airways and began flying people and supplies into and out of the Canadian Arctic. When he was 29, he flew over the barrens of the Northwest Territories, becoming the first to explore the region by air. A year later, he delivered the first airmail to the far reaches of the Arctic, first to Fort Simpson in the Northwest Territories, then later to Aklavik. Because Punch was flying so close to the North Pole, the compass on board his plane malfunctioned. He forged ahead, buzzing over areas of flat, featureless tundra and relying only on his eyesight to keep him on course.

To Punch, nothing was more exciting than flying into uncharted territories—parts of the Canadian north where no mapmakers had ever travelled. On his charts, Punch would see only a vast, white area with an imprecise border. He would set off, filling in the blanks as he went. Often navigating alone

FAST FACT

Punch was one of the movers and shakers behind the development of Edmonton's first airport. Along with some other bush pilots, he convinced the city to pay for the clearing of two pastures north of the city, creating rough runways. He was one of the first two pilots to land there.

over deserted regions, he needed steady nerves and extraordinary endurance. He once flew the entire 3,200-kilometre (2000-mile) route of the Mackenzie River in only two days. On another epic flight, he mapped large parts of the Arctic coastline. Punch was also the first pilot to fly to Great Bear Lake in the Northwest Territories, dropping off some of the prospectors who would later discover uranium along the shores.

Boys Around the World

When he was 20, American Charles Lindbergh quit engineering school, bought his own plane, and became a stunt pilot. In 1927, he made the first non-stop solo flight across the Atlantic Ocean.

In his thirties and forties, Punch managed training schools for World War II pilots, helped manage an airline company, and promoted a new make of bush plane. But even when his work kept him closer to the boardrooms than the barrens, he never stopped flying. In fact, he piloted his own planes until he was 78 years old.

When Punch died in 1995, his son travelled to the Mackenzie River and sprinkled his ashes over the water.

How Will You Rock the World?

When I grow up, I would like to invent a hovercar that would run on water. This would save oil and prevent pollution.

— Palin, age 12

BOYS WHO STOLE THE SPOTLIGHT

ROCKING THE ARTS WORLD

OSCAR PETERSON

PIANIST AND COMPOSER
1925–

Oscar Peterson slipped onto the stage of the auditorium, slid behind the piano, and opened his sheet music. He'd had the music for months, but he'd been busy with sports and friends and summer relaxation. When he'd finally flipped through the pages two days before, he'd found a dizzying confusion of notes well beyond his ability to read music. Nonetheless, he had turned up with his sister at the examinations for the Conservatory of Music in Montreal.

The judges asked him to play the first piece. He tried, but he was soon tangled in the notes and forced to stop.

The judges asked for a second piece, and the same thing happened.

Wondering why someone who had obviously not practised would bother turning up for the audition, the judges asked the young teen what he had been doing with his time.

"I was busy playing another kind of music," he said.

"What kind of music?"

"Jazz."

Fortunately for Oscar, the judges were willing to listen to him play his own selections. After hearing two samples, then finding that he had perfect pitch, they awarded him a passing grade. His older sister, who had spent the entire summer studying, failed the exam.

*

Oscar had been playing the piano since he could remember, taught at first by his father. By the age of 10, he had outstripped his father's knowledge, cast off one instructor as too easy to please, and been told by another that he needed more specialized instruction. By the time he was 14, he was playing in a local jazz band. His sister entered him in an amateur radio competition and when he won, he was given his own weekly 15-minute show.

FAST FACT

Oscar grew up at a time when most black men in Montreal worked for the railway, and certainly didn't play in orchestras. His success in music broke some of the city's racial barriers.

Oscar was feeling quite proud of his achievements until his father came home one day with a new recording. The music was so quick and so perfectly executed that Oscar was convinced his dad was trying to trick him—it was obviously two pianists on the recording, not one. When his dad revealed that one blind musician named Art Tatum was responsible for the performance, Oscar was crushed. He felt that his talent would never measure up, and he quit playing for almost a month.

When he finally rallied, he found himself more eager to learn from experienced band leaders and pianists. He was soon playing with a small orchestra and taking lessons from a new instructor. By 1949, he had formed his own trio and was playing at upscale Montreal dance clubs where only white musicians were usually invited.

BOYS AROUND THE WORLD

German composer Felix Mendelssohn began studying music composition in 1817, when he was eight years old. He appeared in his first concert when he was nine and published his first original work at 13. By the time he was 14, he had produced a dozen symphonies.

In 1949, Oscar was invited to play at Carnegie Hall. Because of union problems and the lack of a work permit for Oscar, the hall manager didn't advertise the event. Instead, rumours of his upcoming appearance spread through the music community. On the chosen night, the manager seated Oscar in the audience. Then, partway through the concert, he announced that he had just "happened" to notice the pianist in the crowd and invited him on stage to play. The concert was a spectacular success.

In the 1950s, Oscar finally met his piano idol Art Tatum, and the two musicians became good friends.

While still playing with a jazz trio, Oscar embarked on a long recording career, playing on more than 80 albums. In the 1960s, he published his first original composition and helped open a school for Canadian musicians. In the following years, towns across America declared official Oscar Peterson days, the government of Canada appointed him to the Order of Canada and presented him with a Governor General's award, and Austria issued a postage stamp in his honour.

A stroke in 1993 left Oscar temporarily unable to play, but after two years of rehabilitation, he was back to composing, performing, and recording. He earned a Grammy for Lifetime Achievement in 1997.

I've always wanted to be a PlayStation 2 disc maker, because I always thought that it was a good way to take up time when you have nothing to do.

— *Brendan, age 7*

LESLIE MCFARLANE

WRITER
1902–1977

High school student Leslie McFarlane stood in front of a burning house, notepad in hand. Sirens wailed their way nearer, and he jumped off the road to avoid a fire truck. A few minutes later, he jumped again after getting completely soaked by a firehose. But to Leslie, every minute was worth it. After months of writing community notes for the local paper, he was getting his first major scoop.

Finding the fire chief amid the chaos, he peppered the man with questions. What could have caused the fire? How long would it take them to extinguish the blaze? The fire chief gave him an ear-searing lecture about interfering in the middle of an emergency, but Leslie continued his note-taking.

A few days later, the story of the fire—his first major piece—was published in the weekly paper. And a week after that, the paper published an apology, because Leslie had gotten the address wrong.

Despite his early fact-checking problems, Leslie showed promise as a writer. He won a historical essay contest when he was 13, a collegiate literary contest when he was 17, and two more literary contests before he finished high school. When he graduated, he began working as a journalist in northern Ontario, then moved to the United States.

He was 23 years old and working at a newspaper in Springfield, Massachusetts, when an advertisement caught his eye. It read:

EXPERIENCED FICTION WRITER WANTED
TO WORK FROM
PUBLISHER'S OUTLINES

Without knowing anything else about the job, Leslie sent away an application. And three weeks later, a proposal arrived in the mail. If Leslie would write two sample chapters of an adventure story for children, according to an outline supplied by the publisher, he could have a chance at finishing the book and receiving $100.

Within days, Leslie had sent away his two sample chapters. Without even waiting for a reply from the publisher, he typed out five more. And when he eventually did receive approval for the book, he worked until after midnight every night for a week, hammering out his first action-filled story.

With his $100 in hand and a promise of more books to come, Leslie quit his newspaper job and moved back to Canada. He made himself at home in a cabin near Sudbury, Ontario. There, he could spend a few hours each morning typing the adventure stories that would pay his rent, then devote the rest of his days to developing his own ideas for more serious literature.

After producing several of Leslie's adventure stories, the publisher turned to detective works. He proposed that Leslie take the pen name Franklin W. Dixon and work on a series about two young

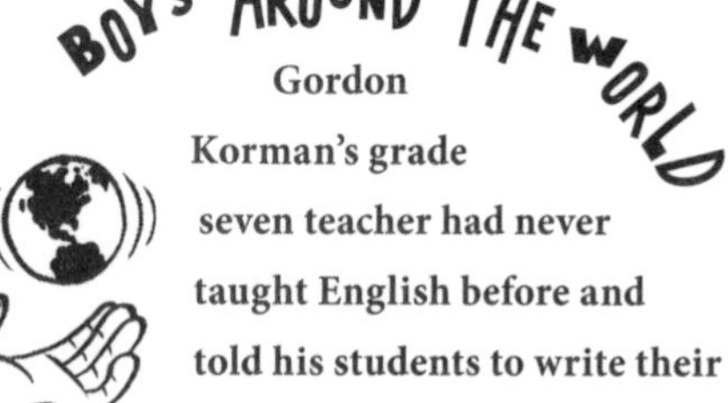

Gordon Korman's grade seven teacher had never taught English before and told his students to write their own novels. The 12-year-old Montreal native earned a B+ for his work, ***This Can't Be Happening at Macdonald Hall*****, and submitted it to Scholastic Books, who published it when Gordon was 14. He's now the author of more than 55 books.**

sleuths, Frank and Joe Hardy. These boys from Bayport on the Atlantic Coast were the sons of a famous private investigator, and though Leslie didn't know it when he rolled his first blank page into his typewriter, they were destined to solve countless mysteries.

The Hardy Boys series would become the world's bestselling collection of children's mystery books. There were 58 titles in the original series, followed by 131 in a newer digest series. Leslie wrote a total of 19 of the titles, establishing the characters, the style of the novels, and their popularity.

But when Leslie began writing the series, he signed a contract giving up any rights to make royalties off the books or to use his real name in association with them. Leslie was happy to sign—he considered the books a side job, and was pleased no one would associate them with his real name. In fact, Leslie didn't even realize how successful the books had become until years later, when his son discovered that he was the author.

"Why didn't you ever tell me?" his son exclaimed.

Leslie was shocked to discover that the books were popular with his son's friends—and selling hundreds of copies at the local bookstores.

Although he made only about $5,000 off books that earned millions, Leslie considered the Hardy Boys series as having been a convenient source of income at the time, and said he didn't mourn any lost royalties. Later in his career, he worked for the National Film Board of Canada and was nominated for an Academy Award. He then moved to Hollywood to write for the TV series "Bonanza."

JIM CARREY

COMEDIAN

1962–

Fourteen-year-old Jim Carrey could hear the blood beating in his ears as he walked onto the stage at Yuk-Yuk's Komedy Kabaret in Toronto. The city's first comedy club was actually just a local community centre, transformed with spotlights, a backdrop, and a swirl of small tables. Each week, one paid professional comic would perform, along with five or ten amateurs.

In 1976, one of those amateurs was Jim. He was used to performing for friends and family, but standing on stage felt incredibly different. When he tried a few impressions of famous people and didn't get many laughs from the crowd, he began to panic. With good reason—Yuk-Yuk's had a cruel way of getting rid of uninspiring comics. After a few minutes, one of the managers reached over with a large hook, snagged it on Jim's waist, and pulled him offstage. Meanwhile, above the recorded sounds of a car crash, the announcer said, "Yes! It's another Yuk-Yuk's disaster!"

For many aspiring comics, that kind of rejection at 14 would have put an end to all thoughts of a career. But as the youngest of four children, Jim had grown up knowing that silliness and crazy jokes were a sure way to gain attention. He'd already perfected his role as the class clown at school.

One of Jim's elementary school report cards reads: "Jim finishes his work first and then disrupts the class." But not all of his teachers discouraged him. One was so impressed by his imitations that she invited him to perform at the Christmas assembly. Another promised that if he worked well all day, he could put on a routine for the class every afternoon, an opportunity that Jim loved.

Maybe Jim needed to keep making jokes because life at home was so difficult: after several years of working together at a local factory under nightmarish conditions, the family quit and spent eight months living out of a camper van. Jim quit school at 16 and got a job at a picture frame factory, but his constant joking cut into his production, and he was fired after six months.

Jim was convinced there was something better than factory work in store for him. With his father's encouragement, he made an appearance in a local telethon and performed a comedy act at a Scarborough restaurant. Then, he went back for a second try at Yuk-Yuk's Komedy Kabaret.

Armed with several more years of practice, Jim managed to overcome his stage fright and crack up the audience with his impressions and contortions. Within just a few months, he'd moved from the amateur spot to paid performances. And at the age of 17, he decided to go for the big time—he moved to Los Angeles and began performing at a popular club there. It didn't take long for his big break to arrive. Rodney Dangerfield was in the audience one night and was so impressed by Jim's act that he invited the teen to open for him during his next tour.

Jim was so determined to be a comedian that he mailed his resume to "The Carol Burnett Show" when he was 10 years old.

Jim was on his way to comedy fame. In 1981, he appeared in his first film. Then, in 1994, he earned international attention with his role in *Ace Ventura, Pet Detective*. He went on to appear in *The Mask*, *Dumb*

Boys Around the World

British actor Daniel Radcliffe appeared in his first movie when he was 10. That same year, he competed against thousands of other actors and won a starring role in one of the most popular children's movies in history—*Harry Potter and the Sorcerer's Stone*.

and Dumber, *Batman Forever*, *Liar Liar*, and *Fun with Dick and Jane*. He also expanded his acting resume to include more serious roles.

Now one of the highest-paid comedic actors in Hollywood, Jim has certainly achieved his childhood dreams.

How Will You Rock the World?

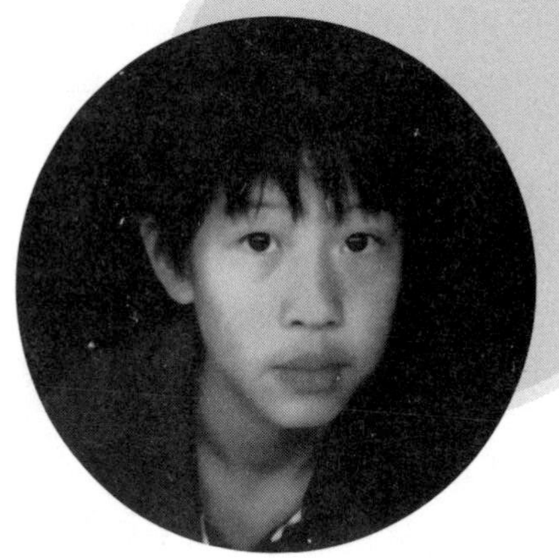

If I could rock the world,
I would become an actor.
I would be a comedian like Jim Carrey or John Candy. I would win many awards such as the Oscars. Then I would retire as a very wealthy man.

— James, age 12

Paul Anka

Singer and Songwriter

1941–

Thirteen-year-old Paul Anka had probably been in more nightclubs than any other teenager in Ottawa. His band, the Bobbysoxers, even performed at a bar where the servers were topless—the manager made Paul wait in the dressing room between acts.

When he wasn't performing with the Bobbysoxers, Paul would often wait for his parents to fall asleep, then sneak out of the house and "borrow" his mother's car. He knew that some of the local nightclubs hosted amateur nights where his smooth voice and teen-idol looks would give him a good chance of success.

Unfortunately for Paul, a late-night engine problem on the middle of a city bridge forced him to call home and confess to his midnight excursions. His parents weren't amused, especially since the young teen didn't even have his driver's licence yet.

Paul took piano lessons and sang in an elementary school choir, but it was thanks to his first shorthand class in high school that his career beckoned to him. Shorthand, he decided, was the most boring subject in the world. Since a music class was offered in the same time period, Paul was soon playing the drums, trumpet, and piano, and developing a love for performance.

As soon as he had tasted show business, Paul grew determined to escape Ottawa and find fame. He even spent an entire season collecting Campbell's soup can labels, all to win a contest that would send him on a free trip to New York.

When he was 15, Paul convinced his parents to let him spend the summer with an uncle in Los Angeles. While working part-time selling candy at a theatre, Paul spent every spare moment contacting recording studios. Eventually, one of them agreed to produce a song. Thrilled, Paul made his recording, returned to Canada, and waited for his star to rise. But despite several TV appearances, the record flopped. Paul was back to touring the local clubs, taking journalism classes to please his father, and waiting for another big break.

It arrived when he was 16. Paul had written a song called "Diana," about his crush on an older girl, and given it to some friends in New York. Eventually, the song sheet made its way to the desk of a record producer. When the producer called to ask for a demo record, Paul was so excited that he drove down from Ottawa himself. After hearing him play, the producer called in his father—to sign a recording contract with ABC-Paramount.

"Diana" was released in 1957 and sold more than 10 million copies. Paul released four more songs the same year that made it to the Top 20 charts, and he was soon touring the world singing in front of audiences of screaming, swooning teenage girls. He performed with Buddy Holly, Chuck Berry, and Jerry Lee Lewis, and headlined at a Las Vegas hotel—all before the age of 20.

BOYS AROUND THE WORLD

Nineteen-year-old Buddy Holly performed onstage with Elvis Presley and signed his first recording contract a few months later. He was soon touring the world and impressing musicians like John Lennon and Paul McCartney. (Buddy's band name "The Crickets" was partly what inspired them to name their group "The Beatles.") But Buddy's career was cut tragically short: he died in a plane crash on February 3, 1959, at the age of 22.

When he wasn't performing, Paul was constantly writing new songs. He created the lyrics for one of Buddy Holly's hits, wrote the theme song for Johnny Carson's "Tonight Show," and composed a song for the movie *The Longest Day.*

FAST FACT

Paul composed songs and recorded albums in Japanese, German, French, and Italian as well as in English.

Paul was achieving his show-business dreams and embarking on a career that would span decades. By 2005, he had written 900 songs, recorded 125 records, and produced 22 Top 20 hits. In his 60s, with five daughters and three grandchildren, Paul was still eager to experiment with music, singing songs that ranged from Van Halen's "Jump" to Nirvana's "Smells Like Teen Spirit."

Through several decades of stardom, the once-exuberant teen never lost his sense of fun.

HOW WILL YOU ROCK THE WORLD?

To rock the world, I would rock the world, literally. I would play awesome rock shows with my guitar for all people. I will ask for donations and I will donate all the money to the homeless in countries everywhere. I will have shows on every continent, with lyrics that would give people hope. Everyone on earth would be rocking out.

— Greg, age 12

Yousuf Karsh

Photographer
1908–2002

British Prime Minister Winston Churchill was on his way from the Canadian Parliament to a security meeting, and Yousuf Karsh learned he would be allowed two minutes to snap his portrait. World War II was beginning, and Yousuf couldn't miss the opportunity to capture one of Europe's greatest leaders. But only two minutes!

Churchill was in no mood to have his photo taken. He was tired and busy and he glowered at Yousuf as the photographer turned on his floodlights. To Yousuf, it seemed like the great politician was glaring at him the same way he would glare at enemy troops.

The prime minister glared even harder when Yousuf asked him to remove the cigar from his mouth. Getting no other response, Yousuf scurried forward, snatched away the cigar, and snapped the photo.

Churchill was so shocked that he actually allowed the photographer to take a second portrait, growling, "You can even make a roaring lion stand still to be photographed."

That image of Churchill, along with his portraits of Albert Einstein, Helen Keller, and Ernest Hemingway, would earn Yousuf a reputation as one of the foremost portrait artists of the 20th century.

*

Yousuf's parents were Armenian, but he was born in Mardin, Turkey, where his father ran an import-export business. As a minority family in the midst of a war, they were persecuted and starved. When they were finally allowed to leave Turkey, Yousuf's parents led their children on a 29-day caravan trek to the Syrian border, abandoning their worldly goods.

When Yousuf was 16, he was sent to Canada to live with his Uncle Nakash, a well-known photographer in Sherbrooke, Quebec. He spent six months in the local school, mostly to learn English, before joining his uncle's business as an apprentice. There, in his uncle's studio, he discovered another world. Along with the developing process, Yousuf learned about taking portraits, about lighting subjects, about bantering with clients until they were comfortable having their photos taken. With a secondhand camera from his uncle, Yousuf began taking his own photographs as well.

Particularly pleased with one of his landscape photos, Yousuf gave a copy to his friend. Secretly, his friend entered it in a contest at a major department store. Yousuf was shocked to open the mail a few weeks later and discover that he'd won the $50 first prize in a contest he hadn't even entered. He immediately gave $10 to his friend and sent the remaining $40 to his family in Syria.

Meanwhile, Yousuf's uncle was seeing more and more evidence of Yousuf's talent and arranged for the boy to work as an apprentice with a famous Boston photographer named John H. Garo. After studying there, then with his uncle again, and finally with a photographer in Ottawa, Yousuf opened a studio of his own. In only six months, he was turning a profit, dating an aspiring actor named Solange Gauthier, and taking portraits of her colleagues in the theatre crowd.

One of his new friends from the theatre was Lord Duncannon, the son of the Governor General of Canada. After tentatively broaching the idea, Yousuf was thrilled to hear that the Governor General and his wife had agreed to come to his studio and have their portraits taken. But the young photographer was so nervous that he found himself barely able to communicate, let alone focus the camera. The portraits were a disaster.

FAST FACT

Yousuf's subjects included Queen Elizabeth II, Fidel Castro, Pope John Paul II, Muhammad Ali, and Walt Disney.

When he could bring himself to admit the problem to Lord Duncannon, he was shocked to find the famous couple at his studio again, graciously allowing him a second try. The new portraits were hugely successful—one of the first major stepping stones in Yousuf's career.

Slowly, along with a thriving business, Yousuf also built a community of family and friends in his new country. His brother Malak followed him to Canada. After World War II, Yousuf was able to sponsor his parents and two other brothers. His wife Solange died in 1961, but Yousuf later married Estrellita Nachbar, whom he met while taking a portrait of her boss, a famous surgeon.

Constantly looking for new ways to expose the personalities of his subjects, Yousuf became famous for his careful staging and lighting. In many cases, he lit his subjects' hands separately, or left parts of their faces in shadow. Today, in photography classes across North America, students copy his techniques.

In 1992, after more than 60 years of work, Yousuf closed his studio. He had photographed 15,000 famous people, becoming famous himself in the process.

BOYS AROUND THE WORLD

Spanish artist Pablo Picasso is known for co-founding a style of painting called cubism. When he was 14, he applied to the Academy of Fine Arts in Barcelona. The entrance examinations usually took a month; Pablo completed them in a single day.

CASHING IN

ROCKING THE BUSINESS WORLD

WILLIAM HAMILTON MERRITT

INDUSTRIALIST
1793–1862

The cargo ship pitched and rocked on massive ocean swells as hurricane winds swept across the Atlantic. Clutching the sides of his bunk and wondering if he'd live through the journey—the ship had already sprung one leak and seemed likely to split apart at any moment—15-year-old William Hamilton Merritt began to wish he'd chosen another semester of school over a chance to sail with his uncle's shipping company. But then his stubborn streak made him reconsider. The Bahamas lay ahead, then a trip to New York, and what other chance would he have if he turned this one down? He concentrated on the thought of palm trees and sugar plantations, and gripped his handholds as the ship see-sawed once more.

The son of a Loyalist settler in the Niagara region of Ontario, Hamilton was born on July 3, 1793. Although known for being especially stubborn and independent, he was eager to learn and spent his teenage years (when he wasn't sailing with his uncle) studying everything from Latin and mathematics to land surveying and navigation.

His studies were interrupted by the outbreak of the War of 1812. His father had fought for the British in the American War of Independence, and now Hamilton signed up to side with the British against the Americans once more. He was soon spending much of his time in skirmishes against groups of American soldiers who were harassing families and destroying farms in the region. At one point, Hamilton and his fellow soldiers were out of uniform when they came across a group of young Americans. By pretending to be Americans themselves, the Canadians tricked the soldiers into revealing their plans.

But it was one of Hamilton's most boring war duties that was to prove the most influential. When the 19-year-old and a troop of 20 fellow soldiers were assigned to guard duty just above Niagara Falls, he was amazed by the size and grandeur of the cascades. Below him, 168,000 cubic metres (6 million cubic feet) of water tumbled each minute over the escarpment. And his experience with his uncle's shipping company made Hamilton realize what a massive obstacle the falls were to trade along the Great Lakes.

Once the war was over and Hamilton had spent several years in business, he and two other mill owners set out on a survey expedition to find a way to bring water, and water-power, closer to their hometown of St. Catharines. By 1818, Hamilton had called a town meeting, collected signatures, and petitioned the Upper Canada Legislature for money to build a waterway completely across the Niagara region from Lake Erie to Lake Ontario. Four years later, he was the financial agent of the Welland Canal Company, with a budget of $150,000.

FAST FACT

Hamilton was a well-known abolitionist—someone who believed that slavery should be outlawed. Some of the escaped slaves who left the United States via the Underground Railroad ended up in St. Catharines, Ontario, and Hamilton was active in a society to help them settle in Canada.

Once again, Hamilton's willpower proved useful. Despite money problems, surveying mistakes, and arguments over the route of the canal, he remained determined to see it built. It was no small undertaking. Lacking the power equipment used in construction today, the crews on the Welland Canal worked with shovels, wheelbarrows, horses, and oxen. Up to 1,000 workers at a time were hired to shovel a channel large enough for commercial ships to pass through.

Cholera epidemics slowed the work. Then, on November 9, 1828, a portion of the canal collapsed. Both the engineers and the work crews were forced to begin again. By the time the canal was nearing completion, extra shovels and wheelbarrows had to be gathered up and sold to help pay the construction bills.

But on November 27, 1829, Hamilton's dream materialized as two ships made the first voyage through the Welland Canal. The R.H. *Boughton* and the *Annie and Jane* became the first vessels to bypass Niagara Falls and sail from Lake Ontario to Lake Erie. Crowds of spectators lined the shores to cheer their arrival.

Today, 3,000 ships carrying 40 million tonnes (44 million tons) of cargo pass through the canal each year, a result of Hamilton's vision and his stubborn determination to see it through.

BOYS AROUND THE WORLD

A 15th-century artist, inventor, and engineer, Leonardo da Vinci began painting and sculpting as a child. In 1502, he sketched an arched bridge for the Sultan of Constantinople. The bridge was never built, because the sultan refused to believe that such a large span—360 metres (1080 feet) long—could support itself. Then, in the late 1990s, Norwegian artist Vebjørn Sand saw Leonardo's sketch and began a campaign to bring it to life. The bridge, built on a smaller scale than the one in the original sketch, is now open to pedestrians and cyclists in southern Norway.

ORONHYATEKHA

PHILANTHROPIST

1841–1907

The Prince of Wales was seated with all the pomp and ceremony that 1860 Canada could offer. Around him were gathered the nation's top politicians and most prominent businessmen. And behind them, a large crowd had flocked in to watch the festivities.

Taking a deep breath, 19-year-old Oronhyatekha took the stage. He had been chosen by the chiefs of six native peoples to offer a welcoming speech. The tall, heavyset youth with striking eyes and a deep, rolling voice spoke for only two minutes, but his clarity, his obvious intelligence, and his native background fascinated the prince. Before the day was over, Oronhyatekha had received an invitation to study at Oxford University in Britain. He would be the first native man to enroll there.

Oronhyatekha had already spent much of his life studying. After showing promise at a school for native children near Brantford, Ontario, he moved to Massachusetts to attend secondary school. While he was probably partially supported by his church, he claimed in his autobiography to have paid his own way, working in the evenings. At times, he wrote, he could only afford plain bread to eat, and earned extra money by cutting wood for a local minister, making 40 cents for every cord (about two pickup-truck loads of wood).

After his spectacular appearance before the Prince of Wales and the trip to Oxford that followed, Oronhyatekha married and enrolled at the University of Toronto. He then began aggressively making places for himself in the realm of medicine and in the social world of the day. As he strove to promote his medical practice, he also joined several men's clubs. And in 1878, he was invited to join the Independent Order of Foresters, an organization previously open only to white men.

BOYS AROUND THE WORLD

As a social activist in the 19th century, Oronhyatekha was controversial simply because of his race. In more recent times, French-Lebanese journalist Samir Kassir drew anger (as well as support) both because of his ethnic background and because of his beliefs. He began writing articles for French newspapers when he was 17, campaigning for freedom for Palestinian people and for democracy in Lebanon and Syria. He was assassinated in Beirut in 2005. His killers were never found.

It didn't take long for Oronhyatekha to realize that his new order was in disarray. Its membership was shrinking and its bank accounts were empty. But he was convinced that with his education and ambition, he could turn the organization around. Apparently, his fellow members agreed: by 1881, he was elected Supreme Chief Ranger. He gave up his medical practice, moved to Toronto, and set out to revive the order.

To Oronhyatekha, the Independent Order of Foresters was a group centred around the principles of brotherly love. Using the resources of richer members, the group could act like a non-profit insurance agency to help poor families in need. It could support people without jobs, offer financial aid to families when a breadwinner was injured or killed in a factory accident, or pay for the education of orphans.

Using his own money (the order at the time had only 396 members and was $4,000 in debt), Oronhyatekha began to tour eastern Canada, speaking passionately about the need for people to help one another. His flamboyant, intense performances soon won him support. And with more members to pay more dues, the order was eventually able to offer low-cost life insurance, pension plans, medical benefits, and disability insurance.

Oronhyatekha was phenomenally successful at a time when racism against native people was overt in Canada. (In fact, according to some biographers, he was about to retire when he heard that some of his members wanted him to leave because of his native heritage. To spite them, he decided to stay on for another term.) Throughout his life, Oronhyatekha spoke the Mohawk language at home and gave lectures about the importance of education for native young people.

But Oronhyatekha's charitable activities reached far beyond the native community. He reigned as Supreme Chief Ranger for 26 years, and during that time the order gave more than $20 million to 100,000 needy people. No other organization, including the Canadian government, offered so much money to the poor.

FAST FACT

Oronhyatekha loved to collect oddities during his travels. His office housed native artwork and artifacts, stuffed birds, an Egyptian mummy, and a replica of the chair where British king Edward VII was crowned.

By the end of Oronhyatekha's tenure, the once-tiny Independent Order of Foresters boasted 45,000 members and a $65,000 surplus. Today, the organization has more than a million members around the world.

HOW WILL YOU ROCK THE WORLD?

If I could rock this world
I would open academies
in South Africa for the poor
children who are suffering. The
academies will provide food, shelter,
clothing, water, and education. The
kids will not be sold for child labour
and will have a place to call home.

— *Eugene, age 12*

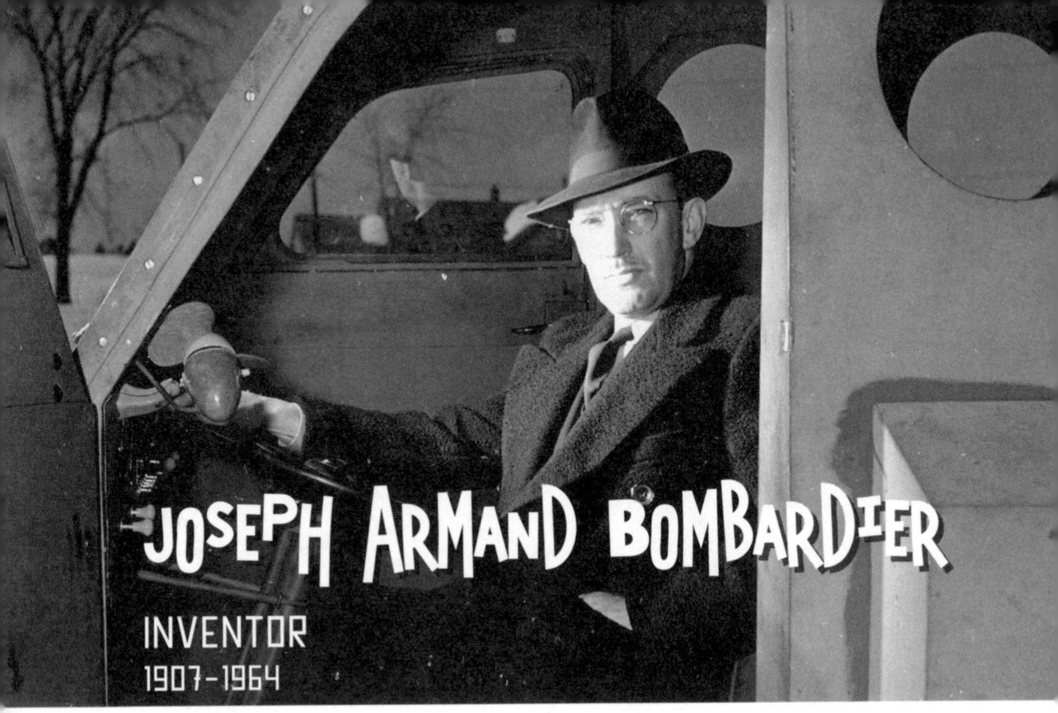

JOSEPH ARMAND BOMBARDIER

INVENTOR
1907–1964

"This is it!" shouted Armand Bombardier.

With the wind whistling around him, Armand drove his newest invention along the roads near his village, through the ditches, and over the embankments. He roared up steep hillsides and careened back down. The local villagers stopped to stare. They were used to Armand coming up with new contraptions, but this one was the strangest yet. It looked like a bathtub mounted on a conveyor belt, with skis and handlebars in the front. And inside, the 52-year-old inventor sat laughing like a young boy.

"This is the snowmobile I've tried to invent all my life!"

Ever since he was a nine- or ten-year-old boy in Vancourt, Quebec, Armand had loved to play with machines. He'd spent hours leaning over the engines of his father's farm vehicles, watching his uncles tinker with the motors. Later, he'd done the tinkering himself. Soon, he was so good at fixing them that he could coax the engines to life in the middle of winter, when no one else could.

Armand's interest in engines led him to a job at the local church, where he could earn enough to buy bits and pieces of equipment from the watch repair shop. Using the tiny springs and gears, he could create model cars and motorboats that actually worked.

Impressed by his son's intelligence, Armand's father arranged for him to attend a nearby religious school. But Armand was bored learning Latin and Greek. All he cared about was machines. So he spent his spare time in the garage with his younger brother, devising his masterwork.

One afternoon when he was 15, he was finally ready to test his invention. With an enormous roar, he and his brother burst from the garage and onto the snowy roadway, driving a huge, heavy farmer's sleigh. Armand had modified the sleigh by adding an engine and a radiator from an old Model T Ford. Then he'd attached a hand-carved wooden propeller, and zoom . . . the two boys were barrelling through the snowdrifts. There was only one problem—his brother didn't quite have the strength to manage the steering cables. After a kilometre-long joyride, they smashed into the side of a neighbour's barn.

Armand's father was furious. They could have hurt themselves or someone from the village. He ordered them to take the sleigh apart immediately. But Armand's dream of building the ideal snow vehicle was born.

A year later, Armand finally convinced his father to let him leave school. He became an apprentice to a mechanic in Montreal. He soaked up all the knowledge he could and spent his after-work hours taking correspondence courses in mechanics and electrical engineering. He taught himself to read English so he could pore over science and technology magazines. He even took an aviation mechanics course, although he didn't have access to a plane.

When he was 19, Armand was ready to move back to his village and open his own garage. To his delight, owning his own business gave him the freedom to experiment with his mechanical ideas. One week, he moved the wheels of an old car closer together and added chains to the back tires, so the car could travel along the tracks of compact snow left by horse-drawn sleighs. The year he turned 20, he modified his design to include skis in the front and double wheels in the back. The winters of Quebec were treacherous, and the vehicles of the time just couldn't travel on the snow- and ice-coated roads. Armand was determined to change that.

His determination increased after his family was struck by tragedy. In 1929, Armand had married a local girl named Yvonne Labreque. (His friends joked that Yvonne was the only girl who would put up with Armand's fast driving.) The couple had a daughter, then a son.

BOYS AROUND THE WORLD

Like Armand, American engineer Henry Ford showed an early aptitude for mechanics and built his first steam engine when he was 15. He later founded the Ford Motor Company, the first manufacturer to use an assembly line to build automobiles. The Model T Ford was released in 1908.

One day, when his son was two years old, Yvonne called Armand at work and asked him to come home immediately. Their tiny son, Yvon, was in terrible pain. The doctor arrived soon after, but there was nothing he could do. The boy needed a hospital, and the closest one was 34 kilometres (21 miles) away in Sherbrooke. Huge snowdrifts covered the roads, and there was no way through. Yvon died of acute appendicitis.

Filled with grief, Armand returned to his workshop, more driven than ever to create a vehicle that could handle all kinds of winter weather. His first breakthrough was the B-7, a seven-passenger bus-like vehicle that ran on skis and a belt, similar to the ones used on today's snowmobiles. Soon, Armand had enough orders that he could close down his garage and dedicate himself to making snow vehicles full-time.

His inventions didn't stop there. During World War II, he created giant troop carriers. Then he travelled across Canada to see what kind of vehicles might be needed in different places. In the west, he developed a winch system to help loggers remove timber from the forest. After hearing

FAST FACT

In the United States and Canada, about four million people ride snowmobiles. Some, such as forestry surveyors, use them for work. Others use them just for fun. Armand himself competed in Ski-Doo competitions, standing on the running boards and racing through the snow.

stories about locomotives sinking in the swamps of the prairies, he created a giant, all-terrain vehicle for oil companies and construction firms.

Then Armand turned his attention to the needs of trappers and hunters working in the Canadian north. They were still using dogsleds or snowshoes for transportation. Soon, he had created the small, durable vehicle that he test-drove through the hills and ditches of his hometown. He called it his Ski-Dog, and it could go almost anywhere. In fact, it was so much fun to drive that even people who didn't hunt or trap wanted to buy it—just for fun. And it could do so much that Armand eventually changed the vehicle's name to Ski-Doo.

Armand died of stomach cancer when he was only 56, but the company he built lives on. Bombardier is still partially owned by Armand's family and employs almost 60,000 workers to make trains and airplanes for companies around the world.

HOW WILL YOU ROCK THE WORLD?

When I grow up I want to invent a snowmobile that doesn't take gas. It would take electricity or something like that. It would help save the environment.

— *Spencer, age 9*

SAM SNIDERMAN

ENTREPRENEUR
1920–

Sam Sniderman watched happily as Buffy Sainte-Marie took the stage to accept an award from the Canadian Music Hall of Fame. The slim native woman was finally gaining fame for her folk and protest songs.

Then Sam almost jumped from his seat. Had she just said what he thought she said? Yes! The people on either side of Sam were smiling at him, leaning over to pat him on the shoulder. She'd just said that Sam the Record Man had been instrumental in her success.

It was Sam's proudest moment. After decades of promoting his favourite Canadian musicians and seeing singers like Anne Murray and Joni Mitchell reach international stardom, he was thrilled to feel he had played a key role in their careers.

Raised by a single mother, who taught him the basics of business in her dry-goods store, Sam had originally planned to become a lawyer. But at 17, his classes seemed like drudgery. He knew that his family couldn't afford university tuition, anyway. He dropped out of school before writing his final exams and signed on at his brother Sid's store—Sniderman Radio Sales and Service.

Sam was soon proficient at radio repair, but it wasn't the most exciting or prosperous business. Eager to do something more glamorous, he persuaded his brother to clear a corner of the store for music sales. Of course, there were no CDs at the time; Sam wanted to sell records. To appeal to the new immigrants living in the neighbourhood, he stocked the store with his own favourites as well as a good selection of foreign performers.

Soon, the record business was squeezing out the radio repair shop. The brothers moved to a bigger store, then an even bigger downtown Toronto location. And Sniderman Radio Sales and Service became Sniderman's Music Hall, then, with much persuasion from Sid, Sam the Record Man.

By 1969, Sam was ready to expand again. He and Sid created the Sam the Record Man franchise, allowing other owners to open their own Sam the Record Man stores across the country. It was the first franchised record business in North America.

As his success grew, Sam dedicated himself to expanding and fostering the Canadian music industry, volunteering with the Toronto Arts Council, the Hamilton and Region Arts Council, the East Coast Music Association, the National Theatre School, and Ontario's Humber College. He helped to establish a library of recordings at the University of Toronto and worked with the Canadian National Exhibition to choose each year's main music attractions.

Sam's limitless energy paid off. By the 1980s and '90s, there were more than 130 Sam the Record Man stores in Canada. Up to one-fifth of all records bought in Canada were bought at one of Sam's stores. He was inducted into the Order of Canada and honoured at the Canadian Country Hall of Fame and the Juno Awards.

FAST FACT

In the 1990s, Sam was astonished to learn that his son and niece had created a cutting-edge website for the record chain. Sam himself had never learned to use the store computers.

Both Sam and his brother loved the day-to-day work of the record store. Sid was still reporting to his office when he was 93, and Sam loved helping people discover new acts. But by the late 1990s, the personal touch

Boys Around the World

Michael Dell started a computer company from his university dorm room. It was so successful that he dropped out of school at 19, borrowed some money from his grandparents, and founded Dell Computer Corporation. He is now the fourth-richest man in the United States.

of the Sam the Record Man stores couldn't compete with the glitzy displays and huge buying power of international music chains. Sam handed the reins of the business over to his son Jason and his niece Laura, but they were unable to turn the trend around. In 2001, the chain declared bankruptcy.

In 2002, Jason and Laura managed to reopen the flagship store in downtown Toronto, and the name Sam the Record Man lives on.

How Will You Rock the World?

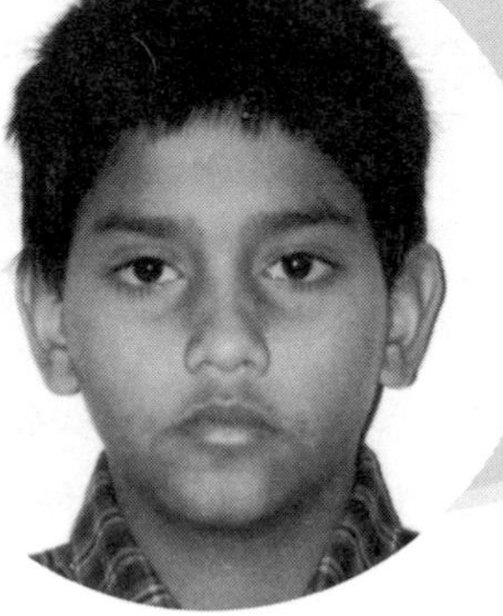

I want to be a lawyer. My parents always told me that I am argumentative. They told me I can twist sentences to change meanings.

— *Shikhar, age 12*

SAMUEL CUNARD

INDUSTRIALIST
1787–1865

Fourteen-year-old Samuel Cunard picked every dandelion leaf he could find. Then he bundled the greens and carted them down to the local market, where he sold them. They weren't worth much, but he earned enough to scramble down to the Halifax wharves that week and bargain with the traders who auctioned their goods there. Sam found a few good deals on coffee and spices. Then he bundled those up and began going door to door along the streets near his house, selling his new wares.

From dandelion leaves to money to coffee and back to more money—Sam's days of wheeling and dealing were just beginning. By the time he was 17, Sam's older sister had married a navy officer and moved to England. His older brother had gone to sea, eager to become a ship's captain one day. Sam, too, saw ships in his future. But he didn't want to sail them—he wanted to own them. He began working for his father's shipbuilding company, learning the basics of the trade. He then travelled to Boston to apprentice in a ship broker's office.

At 20, Sam returned home. Although his father was still officially in charge of the business, it was soon Sam who made all the important decisions. And when the War of 1812 broke out between Britain and the United States, it was Sam who helped arrange for the Cunard family ships to fly neutral flags and continue their trade up and down the coast. Their steamships arrived in the Halifax port laden with rum and molasses, sugar and coffee. By the end of the war, with a successful trading company, the newly married Sam was one of Halifax's most respected businessmen.

FAST FACT

Sam's company eventually became the Cunard White Star Line, which owns the ocean liners *Queen Elizabeth 2* and *Queen Mary 2*, some of the largest luxury passenger ships in the world.

Although he loved making money, Sam also spent plenty of time giving it away. He was one of two local leaders selected by the government to help poor immigrants arriving in Halifax after the war. With his partner, he helped place new families in communities where jobs were available, and he set up a soup kitchen for the city's poor. It was obviously needed: it went through 455 litres (100 gallons) of soup each day.

Meanwhile, as Sam's steamers carried goods and mail and expensive tea between Halifax, Boston, London, and Bermuda, the business continued to grow. Between 1817 and 1850, he bought 76 ships. Some he resold at higher prices, and others he used for trade. He continued to win contracts and gain the respect of other traders because of his record for safety and reliability: his ships arrived where and when they were supposed to.

Always alert to new opportunities, Sam often dabbled in other areas of business, including mining, timber, and real estate. (At one point, he owned one-seventh of Prince Edward Island.) But it was in his main area of interest, shipping, that he began

BOYS AROUND THE WORLD

Japanese businessman Takafumi Horie started a website design company with some college friends and expanded his business interests, becoming CEO of the Internet company Livedoor and a director of Fuji Television. He has recently opened a private space exploration business with hopes to launch a Japanese rocket.

to see exciting new opportunities. In the 1830s and '40s, steamships began to replace wooden sailing ships along the coast. Sam was quick to see that the new ships could carry goods faster than ever before. When his first steamship, the *Britannia*, sailed from London to Boston in 1840, the businesspeople and high-society citizens of Boston were so impressed that Sam received 1,800 invitations to dinner. The sailing marked the opening of the first trans-Atlantic cargo and passenger steamship service.

By the time Sam died in 1865, his company owned a fleet of ships that travelled the coast and criss-crossed the Atlantic. He left his estate to his two sons and six daughters. They settled in England to enjoy their wealth.

HOW WILL YOU ROCK THE WORLD?

I would like to rock the world by founding my own video game studio. I would make fresh, original games that aren't based on violence. This will decrease the crime rate among teenagers.

— Nabil, age 12

Acknowledgements

I would like to thank the staff of the Vancouver Public Library, Library and Archives Canada, and the Canadian War Museum for their help with the research and photo editing for this project. I would also like to thank the following individuals for their time and advice: Heidi Brown, Laury Heydon-O'Neil, Emery Leger, Erin McMillan, and Chris Webster. A big thank you to all the students who submitted ideas about how they would rock the world.

Selected Sources

Brawn & Brains

Buffery, Steve. "Elvis' New Move Rocks Skating World." *Toronto Sun*. March 15, 1991.

Cosentino, Frank, and Don Morrow. *Lionel Conacher*. Don Mills: Fitzhenry & Whiteside, 1981.

Gretzky, Wayne, and Rick Reilly. *Gretzky*. Toronto: HarperCollins, 1990.

Hansen, Rick, and Jim Taylor. *Rick Hansen*. Vancouver: Douglas & McIntyre, 1987.

"Rick's Story" from the website of the Rick Hansen Man in Motion Foundation: www.rickhansen.com.

Stojko, Elvis. *Heart and Soul*. Toronto: Rocketeer, 1997.

Weider, Ben. *The Strongest Man in History*. Vancouver: Mitchell, 1976.

Wicked Warriors

Andrews, Allen. *Brave Soldiers, Proud Regiments*. Vancouver: Ronsdale, 1997.

Eckert, Allan W. *A Sorrow in Our Heart*. New York: Bantam, 1992.

Maclaren, Roy. *Canadians Behind Enemy Lines, 1939–1945*. Vancouver: UBC Press, 2004.

Quan, Holly. *Sam Steele*. Canmore, Alberta: Altitude, 2003.

Steele, Sam. *Forty Years in Canada*. Toronto: Prospero, 2000.

Sudgen, John. *Tecumseh*. New York: Henry Holt, 1997.

Uncommon Courage. Ottawa: Veterans Affairs Canada, 1985.

Brainiacs

Clark, Robert Dean. "J. Tuzo Wilson" from the website of the Society of Exploration Geophysicists: www.mssu.edu/seg-vm/bio_j_tuzo_wilson.html.

Fessenden, Helen M. *Fessenden*. New York: Coward-McCann, 1940.

Goldberg, Steve. "Scholastic Chess" from the website ChessCafe.com: www.chesscafe.com/scholastic/scholastic.htm.

Green, Lorne. *Chief Engineer*. Toronto: Dundurn, 1993.

MacLean, Hugh. *Man of Steel*. Toronto: Ryerson Press, 1969.

Raby, Ormond. *Radio's First Voice*. Toronto: Canadian Communications Foundation, 2001.

Young, Gayle. *The Sackbut Blues*. Ottawa: National Museum of Science and Technology, 1989.

TRAILBLAZERS

"Alberta's Aviation Heritage" from the website of the Alberta Aviation Museum: www.abheritage.ca/aviation/people/between_punch_dickins.html.

"Canada's Bush Pilots" from the website of Canada's Digital Collections: Collections.ic.gc.ca/heirloom_series/volume4/76-81.htm.

Davies, K.G. "Henry Kelsey" from the website of the Dictionary of Canadian Biography Online: www.biographi.ca/EN/ShowBio.asp?BioId=34991.

Francis, Daniel. *Discovery of the North*. Edmonton: Hurtig, 1986.

Whillans, James W. *First in the West*. Edmonton: Applied Art Productions, 1955.

BOYS WHO STOLE THE SPOTLIGHT

Karsh, Yousuf. *In Search of Greatness*. Toronto: University of Toronto Press, 1962.

———. *Karsh*. Boston: MFA Publications, 2003.

Knelman, Martin. *The Joker Is Wild*. Toronto: Viking, 1999.

Lees, Gene. *Oscar Peterson*. Toronto: Key Porter, 1988.

McFarlane, Leslie. *Ghost of the Hardy Boys*. Toronto: Methuen/Two Continents, 1976.

Peterson, Oscar. *A Jazz Odyssey*. London: Continuum, 2002.

CASHING IN

Grant, Kay. *Samuel Cunard*. London: Abelard-Schuman, 1967.

"The Inventor: Joseph-Armand Bombardier." *Maclean's*. 4 Sept. 2000: 40.

Merritt, J.P. *Biography of the Hon. W.H. Merritt*. St. Catharines: E.S. Leavenworth, Book and Job Printing Establishment, 1875.

Oronhyatekha, M.C. *History of the Independent Order of Foresters*. Toronto: Hunter, Rose, 1894.

"Oronhyatekha." From the website of the Dictionary of Canadian Biography Online: www.biographi.ca/EN/ShowBio.asp?BioId=41098.

Precious, Carole. J. *Armand Bombardier*. Markham, Ontario: Fitzhenry & Whiteside, 1984.

Williams, Jack. *Merritt*. St. Catharines: Stonehouse, 1985.

PHOTO CREDITS

BRAWN & BRAINS

Louis Cyr: photo (detail) courtesy of the National Archives of Canada, C-086343.

Elvis Stojko: photo (detail) by F. Scott Grant, courtesy of Skate Canada.

Lionel Conacher: (based on) photo courtesy of the National Archives of Canada, PA-047102.

Rick Hansen: photo (detail) courtesy of the Rick Hansen Man in Motion Foundation.

Wayne Gretzky: photo (detail) by Barry Gossage, courtesy of the Pheonix Coyotes.

WICKED WARRIORS

Alan Arnett McLeod: (based on) photo courtesy of the Canadian War Museum, 19780702-116.

Thomas Ricketts: photo courtesy of the Canadian War Museum, C-33185.

Sam Steel: photo (detail) courtesy of the National Archives of Canada, PA-204294.

BRAINIACS

Sandford Fleming: (based on) photo courtesy of the National Archives of Canada, C-014238.

Mark Bluvshtein: (based on) photo courtesy of Mark Bluvshtein.

John Tuzo Wilson: (based on) photo courtesy of the Ontario Science Centre.

Hugh Le Caine: photo (detail) courtesy of the National Archives of Canada, PA-167153.

Reginald Fessenden: (based on) photo courtesy of the Canadian Communications Foundation.

TRAILBLAZERS

Simon Jackson: photo courtesy of Simon Jackson.

Joseph Elzéar Bernier: photo (detail) courtesy of the National Archives of Canada, C-025960.

Kozo Shimotakahara: (based on) photo courtesy of the Kootenay Lake Archives, Kaslo, BC.

Clennel Dickins: photo (detail) courtesy of the National Archives of Canada, C-060469.

BOYS WHO STOLE THE SPOTLIGHT

Oscar Peterson: photo (detail) courtesy of the National Archives of Canada, PA-182399.

Paul Anka: photo (detail) courtesy of the National Archives of Canada, PA-202353.

CASHING IN

William Hamilton Merritt: (based on) photo courtesy of the National Archives of Canada, C-057006.

Oronhyatekha: (based on) photo courtesy of The Independent Order of Foresters.

Joseph Armand Bombardier: photo (detail) courtesy of the National Archives of Canada, e000761190.

Sam Sniderman: (based on) photo courtesy of Sam the Record Man.

Samuel Cunard: photo courtesy of the National Archives of Canada, PA-124022.

INDEX

About the Author

Tanya Lloyd Kyi is the author of eight books for children and young adults, including *Canadian Girls Who Rocked the World*, *Fires!*, *Rescues!*, *Jared Lester: Fifth Grade Jester*, and *The Blue Jean Book*, which won the Christie Harris Illustrated Children's Literature Prize. When not writing, she can be found trying to hang onto the disc on the ultimate field or feeding her secret World of Warcraft obsession. She lives in Vancouver with her husband, Min. Their two-year-old daughter Julia has not yet rocked the world, but successfully rocks the house every day.